ISBN 978-1-4452-1397-2 Copyright Language English
Country United Kingdom Publication Date 17 October
2009

Mark Collar was born in West Bridgford, Nottingham and lived within sight of the City Ground until his parents finally tired of him and threw him out. He attended Universities in Liverpool and Sussex to qualify as a teacher. He has taught English in High Schools in Suffolk and Norfolk for more than twenty years. He has always used his writing with his students. He is a keen collector of memorabilia from the First World War, so it seemed natural that his first novel should arise from that era. He is married to a wife who seems far too good for him and has one son.

His writing was first published in the Rushcliffe School magazine in the 1970s. In the early 1980s he wrote three poems that were the centrepiece of a Christmas broadcast on Radio Trent. He is proud of the fact that his poetry has provided epitaphs at the funerals of two people that meant a lot to him. He has had a large number of poems published in the small press and his short story on the first Zeppelin raid attracted the interest of the Great Yarmouth Mercury. In the guise of 'Me Owd Duck' he has a monthly Web page on the 'You've Lost that Loving Feeling' Forest fans forum (ltlf.co.uk) where his character writes about the history of Nottingham Forest Football Club.

Acknowledgements

There has to be a compromise to be made with a book like this between telling the story and finding every detail. I am aware of all those people whose lives seem dedicated to keeping alive the memory of the RFC and its wonderful contribution to the First World War. They have helped me understand so many facets of Ball's story.

The characters in the story are all my own invention, they are based on the people they were, but I could never have known them, so have filled in the details of their stories with as much as I could find about them. Some, like the Balls, were carefully researched. Others, notably the girls on the farm, were made up, based on the stories of other women who suffered through that awful war.

My desire to write the story came through correspondence with Cross and Cockade International. Nick Forder, the Flight and Space curator at the Museum of Technology in Manchester has acted as a reference point throughout my writing. I hope I have managed to accurately convey the RFC as it was.

I soon realised that to understand Ball, I would need to see his plane fly. My deepest thanks are due to Julie Lack-White and the Shuttleworth collection, for allowing me to see, hear and touch an SE5A. I also learned a great deal from its devoted mechanic, John now in his eighties but just the sort of mechanic that Ball would have wanted on his team.

Kim Mycock, at Trent College reacted wonderfully to unscheduled visits; I am in debt to all the people I met at the school for their helpfulness and their commitment to keeping the legend that is Ball alive.

Much of the story comes from the records and letters at the Nottinghamshire archives and I received a great deal of help from the staff there. I must also thank Steve Zaliek, editor of the Lenton Times, for permission to use his research on the Lenton War Memorial for the Gommecourt chapter.

War makes ordinary people do extraordinary things. It also highlights the actions of extraordinary people. It has been a privilege telling their stories.

Albert and Flora
By Mark Collar

1.

Monday May 7th 1917 Vert Galant Aerodrome, Near Douellens, France

These were the days when even the clouds could kill you, and he saw them so often in his dreams. Going into a cloud was entering a rolling mist that could take you to a place where only dreams were real. Thick white clouds wept with mist, which twirled and rose, as if arising from the stagnant battlefield below. Clouds that smelled of cordite fumes, mustard gas, and blood. Clouds that groped leeringly over your wing tops. Clouds that stole your horizons, and your sense of up and down, and side to side. Clouds hiding deadly Huns. As if the whole plane and the man inside were consumed by the mists. Clouds ate you. You would never find the Hun in here, Oh no, he had everywhere to hide. Only the airman knew what was inside the clouds, the mountains and valleys, the pockets of pure clear blue air.

In dreaming, the boy drifted deep in mountains of clouds. In dreams, his plane flew silently, his gun never jammed. With every spurt of fire, the Huns fell in flames, spiralling round and down. Every victory was a kill, clean and true and good.

In dreams, Bobs was waiting on the station platform, tall and willowy with flowers in her hat. She was waving and the band was playing. He saw her tawny hair, her

dark eyes and her smile. His father stood next to her, proudly waving a Union Jack.
The war was over; in dreams, the slaughter ended. But this was not a time for
dreaming.

The boy woke with a start and the clouds instantly dissipated. The first limp ray of
sunlight breaking the mists through the knot holes of the shack illuminated his wrist
watch. Opening its golden grill, designed to protect the face from bullets, he saw that
it was 5am. He leant forward in the dawns light and listened hard. Aside from the
song of a lark, and a rumble of angry distant guns he had long ceased to notice; there
was silence. Neither engine noise nor warning telephone ring had made his waking at
that moment purposeful. His mind had awoken him, in spite of how fagged he felt.
He had carefully trained it to be like this. It was his alarm clock, calendar, and
revolver.

The shack still smelt of burning. His white and blue striped pyjamas were shell
holed with spots of ash. There was oil still clinging to the tip of his left ear. Ball was
frequently speckled with mud or oil all his life. At first, Commanding Officers would
get quite upset about it, but later, it was accepted that he might be the officer with his
hands in his pockets in a photograph, or wearing slippers in uniform or still in
pyjamas in the air; that was Ball. He had thick black hair and eyes that were never
still. His eyes seemed to trace the tails of dragonflies in the sky. They were dark, so
dark sometimes the pupils were hard to find. He was still just a boy, the war was just
his second real job, but it was one he was really good at.

He had reached the stage of still feeling tired as soon as he woke up. There had been
tiredness for as long as he could remember it seemed. It used to be that the moment
the plane's wheels left the ground, he immediately felt awake and alive, ready to do

7

the job. That moment used to be the point when his fatigue lifted but this time in France, it had never gone away. His nerves had been flying next to him like an Observer all this trip. To calm himself he had begun singing her song, almost to drown the noise of the Lewis gun and that ferocious siren wail of the SE5 in a dive. He had always sung in the air and in his garden, but only on this trip to France did he sing her song.

He only ever allowed himself the briefest glimpse of her out here. Those memories were too rich; too precious to be exposed to this place where murder had become a lauded and noble act.

He rubbed his eyes with his hands and sat up. This should be his last day on the job. Despite all his Father's pleadings, the War Office and General Trenchard had allowed him one month and not one day more to achieve his aim. As this was the 31st day of his promised month back at the front, the warrant for his leave should arrive any day. He hoped they'd let him get to fifty victories before it was time to go.

Yet England and Flora felt a very long way away. Leave still seemed to be some other world. He could only focus on his next patrol. When things had been bad in the past, leave had been snatched away from him; and things felt bad again now.

Dreams had always been his downfall. On his last leave, He had this nagging feeling that his last leave would be just that, forever. As he had flown off from London Colney for France last time, he had this overwhelming sensation that he would never land in England again. So many of his friends had gone; how long could anyone hope to go on? Was the shield that he had always known God had placed around him, an eternal one? He thought not.

Throwing off the bedclothes he found his slippers with his feet, and then found a box of matches on the makeshift wooden dresser by the bed. Despite the miracles he and Maxwell had done the day before, most of the shack would need to be rebuilt. The wood was scarred in some places and blistered in others. It smelt burnt and felt damp. It wouldn't survive the autumn rains, let alone the depths of winter exposed out here.

He lifted the thick green tarpaulin that served as a makeshift door and the dawn sunlight blinded him momentarily. Then he saw that the sky was clear as crystal and blue. The French countryside stretched around him, almost as big and as vast as the sky. Here, away from the front, green was still dominant, even over the huts and the hangars of the airfield. This part of France had been spared the carnage. The airfield was at a crossroads. One busy road ran right through it, from North to South. Along this road were the hangars, usually the busiest place on the airfield, but quiet this morning. Along this road, they had watched the men march forwards to the front at Arras, and the women and children, and old men and donkeys, and mules pulling sad tear filled carts, drag themselves back to the hope of Amiens. France had been awash with human litter since the beginning of the war.

The boy surveyed the sky from the doorway, silently thanked God for the good flying weather, and then went in search of cake; Lol's cake, the chocolate one. This was good cake with thick icing and the sponge had stayed moist, despite the distance it had travelled. It was topping cake. He found the metal tin in the gloom then carried it outside. This was the precious Goodies tin. Only the things he liked best were stored in here; cake, chocolates and sweets. He cut the cake with his penknife and ate it quickly. There was no need for haste, the airfield was quiet. His flight's patrol was scheduled for twelve thirty in the afternoon, and many ground crews had worked until

9

late, like he had, the night before. It was the jam problem that had occupied them deep into the night.

The Lewis gun on the SE5 kept jamming, often in the middle of combat with a hostile aircraft; and the last thing you needed was to be facing a HA with no weapons. It meant a chase, at best, back to the British lines. Ball was sure that many of the friends he had lost had fallen whilst trying to deal with a jammed weapon, in a plane that was being asked to fly itself too often. He viewed the Lewis gun as a friend you had to rely on and at the moment, his friend had let him down on several occasions.

Ball's half burnt shack was next to a row of Nissen huts from whence he could hear his ground crew breathing deeply and someone, probably Ted, was snoring contentedly. Ball had managed to find a bottle of cognac for them the night before; in truth he had had it for a week and was waiting for the right time to give it to them, but had waited for some cake to arrive, to go with it.

He did not drink himself; he had listened intently to the sermon some months ago, back at the little chapel in Shenley. The text was: 'Your body is a temple of the Holy Spirit,' and the message was that you should not pollute that temple. Ball felt that as an officer, he had an example to set. In any case, he had given up smoking a year ago for good and he disliked alcohol, one could not drink and fly; but he loved cakes and would take a piece flying with him. All his people knew that.

He went round to the back of his shack to the water heater that was under the tank from the bath and lit it. They had made a good job of putting the thing together. Most of the parts they had used were from planes that no longer flew.

A line of shallow drainage ditches separated the aerodrome from the road. He and Maxwell had been hunting rats there. After the fire, they had seen rats running through the night. They leapt out of their nests under the burning huts and ran for shelter to the ditches. They asked Lewis to act as a beater and run along the ditch. Ball stood armed with his Browning automatic and Maxwell had his Webley service revolver. They had felt like two duellists in a field. As each fat rat ran from the ditch they had swiftly dispatched it. They only missed one between them, although Ball reckoned he shot more than Maxwell. The Browning blew their bodies up higher in the air than the Webley.

Next to his shack grew a garden. There had been a greenhouse as well, but that had gone in the fire, and was now a blackened heap of wood and shattered glass. Albert had done his best to put the garden right again. He had planted rows of peas and marrows, carrots and lettuces. On the way to Bapaume, Albert had seen spring onions growing in an abandoned farmer's field, and had made a mental note to go back there and get some seedlings. The marrows had gone down so well in the Mess; he was convinced the onions would be even better.

The garden was tidy and ordered. Everything had its place and was planted out in straight rows. It was a place of calm in a world of chaos; it was a ground full of birth in a land of death; a heaven where you could hide from war and killing; a place to lose yourself for a few delicious moments. There were a few flowers planted there, sweet peas and geraniums brought from Nottingham, but mostly there were things that would one day be nice to eat; the ground had been given promise. The soil and the sunshine that had soaked up, and looked down on so much death, at last were being used to bring life again.

In the furthest corner of his garden, two red poppies grew. Albert noticed them now, in the dawn's waking light; their black hearts, the frail blood red petals. They grew

11

everywhere here.   They grew in forlorn muddy trenches, with no hope left in sight. They grew on long abandoned farms which had become killing fields. They grew on the backs of old corpses, matted with flies. They grew between the rows of white crosses in Flanders. They grew amongst the desolation and violation that was war. He had not planted them, but he would not pick them, he could not kill them, and he left them to flutter in the breeze.

Monday May 17th 1917 Hacketts Farm, Wood End, Hertfordshire.

The first rays of dawn began to swell under the curtains and Flora knew it was time to start work. She arose and washed her face and hands with the water in the bowl on her dresser. She began brushing her long tawny brown hair first; she did it rhythmically and found it soothing. Then she dressed slowly, deliberately. Her uniform was on the chair next to her and she put on the brown twill breeches, the green jumper and puttees, the wide brimmed green Women's Land Army hat and laced up her hob nailed boots. As she dressed, the other girls with her also woke and began preparing for the day. There were whispered good mornings. Beatrice fussed, Violet busied herself and Amy smiled at Flora. There were four Land Girls in the farmhouse, the same number as the number of sons Farmer Hackett had sent off to the front. Two of those sons were gone now and would never return.

    After two years of war, the Government had realised that so many men had been lost; it would have to ask women to work the land. The harvest was in danger of rotting in the fields. The German naval blockade was beginning to bite and the country had suffered so many losses. Flora had read in the 'Daily News' back last February of the Nation's need for 400,000 women to work the land. Nineteen year old Flora Cavanagh Young had had ideas of becoming an Opera singer and had undergone two years of training; however she was not slow to answer her country's call. She had queued with the other women in St Paul's Churchyard to receive a brief medical. Then she was given a notice to arrive at St Albans Station the following week and take a train to the first of four farms she had worked on.

She drew back the curtains to reveal a cloudless sky and the sun just beginning to rise above the horizon. Then she helped Amy on with her boots, a feat that involved much laughter, as they collapsed on the floor together. There was a quiet hush, as the girls readied themselves for the day and then tramped down the stairs to where Hackett was waiting for them.

'Mornin' Ladies, I wasn't sure you'd be joining us today.' Hackett was gruff and wily. He had worked this land all his life. The day always began, early or late with some remonstration for tardiness, it was his way. His wife had died four years ago and his sons had gone away, he was enjoying the company of the girls. The farm could be a lonely place.

'We waited to see if the weather was fine first'. Flora replied with a wry smile. It was as much humour as she could muster this early in the day. Her boots were uncomfortable and still wet from the day before. The boots were only ever dry after the weekend. The dew came through the holes for the laces.

'We thought it might be nice, for you to milk all forty of them yourself, this morning.' Amy joked. She was a year older than Flora and it showed, although Flora was the tallest of the four girls. Amy's curly blond hair was bundled up beneath her WLA hat, as was the hair of all the girls. All over England, even at this early hour, girls dressed like men were rising to do their work. The girls at Hackett's farm were

13

no different to any others; they followed Hackett out from the farmhouse to the field where the herd stood patiently waiting for them. As soon as the farmer opened the five barred gate, a stream of steaming black and white Friesians, with full ripe udders, made their lumbering way up into the milk shed.

Flora had been terrified of the beasts when she first came to the farm. As a child, her mother had taken her for a long walk in the countryside. Her mother liked to carve wood and they would walk miles together looking for suitable pieces. She had skipped away at one time to find wild flowers and her mother was some way in the distance behind her. She had been crossing an unfamiliar field, when a herd of cows had taken an interest in her. One had come right up close to her and had butted the stick that she carried. She looked at the hard white horns, the hard flat black forehead that hit the stick with a deep threatening sound, and turned and ran as fast she could, back to her mother. She had soon learned from Hackett, that if she had shouted at it, as small as she was, it would have run away. Cows were not very clever creatures.

The girls fell in with the herd and followed their now accustomed routine. Hackett led the cows into the stalls. Flora, Violet and Beatrice each had a stall and sat on a small stool. Their shoulders pressed into the sides of the cow; their fingers neatly pulling the milk from the cow's teats into the pail below. Once each cow had been milked, Amy washed its udder from a brown wooden bucket full of soapy water and then led it back into the yard. They still joked about their first morning milking on the farm. While Hackett showed the others how to coax the milk from the udder, he had asked Amy to wash the first cow he had milked. Setting to work with keen ardour, Amy had washed the cow from head to hoof. As she was cleaning the last hoof Hackett looked up at her and let out a long guffawing laugh.

14

'I meant you to wash the udder, where the milk comes from. If you wash them all, we'll be here all day. Still, 'spose I'll have the cleanest herd in Hertfordshire while you're here'. It had taken Amy a week to get over the joke.

Milking was not hard work but it demanded certain deftness, a certain skill. At the weekend, the girls went home and Hackett was helped by old men from the village. Flora found milking very calming and the girls would strike up conversation as they worked. The atmosphere in the milk shed was warm and bright that May morning. Outside the dawn chorus was building gently, and inside the sound of the milk rhythmically squirting into the three pails was somehow comforting.

Flora rested her forehead on the soft side of the great warm creature. She found it comforting being around them now. She was always careful to relax the animals she milked. She called this one Lady. The first time she had milked her; Lady had stepped back at the wrong moment and down had gone the pail. The precious warm white milk running wasted on the cowshed floor had upset Flora; she could not bear it when things went to waste.

'Your chap's month is up today isn't it Flora?' called Violet from the next stall. 'It should be'. Flora sighed. She chose her words carefully. 'The General said one month and no more but there's no sign of leave in his letters yet'. The last of these she had received the day before. He had said he was longing to see her again which had made her heart beat faster. She knew that longing so well, they had barely had enough time together to really know each other and she wanted so much more of him. She loved to be a part of his intensity.

She was wary of talking about him too much to Violet. Violet had lost both her brother and her fiancé on the same day the previous year; although the news took days to arrive; they had both gone on the big push of July 1st. She had a telegram to say the brother was missing and then the C.O. of her brother's regiment had written to his family, saying that he had died bravely and had not suffered. So many families now owned a letter like that. A letter saying 'died bravely' but no replacement for their father, husband or son. On that one day alone, in this three year old war, twenty thousand letters had needed to be written.

The women that had not lost their lovers were fast becoming a minority. To have lost a lover had become so sadly, deeply normal. There was no family or community that had escaped death. Every one you knew could name a man that had gone; usually their father, lover or son. Thousands had fallen in three years of war that showed no signs of ending.

'You'll be expecting another letter today then.' Flora could detect sadness in Violet's voice for the letters she would never receive.

'Oh, probably not today, he is very busy and doesn't write every day.' This was almost a lie, he had written just about every day, since the day they had met, but the censors and the slow post meant that they tended to arrive at intervals in batches of two or three. His writing sloped and was hard to read, he made up the spellings of words he did not know, but she had letters and was so grateful for them. They were so precious to her. He managed to write her a brief line saying that he missed her after a day of chasing German planes, but that was enough for her.

'I expect he'll whisk you off to marry you and live in a nice big house somewhere when he's back. No more milking for you girl'. Flora grimaced, Violet had often commented on the speed at which her relationship with Albert had taken place.

16

'Introduced one day and engaged the next,' was how she had described it to Amy.

Flora squeezed the black cow's teats with a new urgency.

'Oh no,' Flora replied quickly, 'he's said we'll wait for the end of the war, whenever that might be…' Her voice trailed off into the barn's morning light.

2.

Thursday August 24th 1905. Sedgeley House The Park Nottingham.

'Now Lad, be prepared for the recoil, as soon as the bullet discharges from the chamber, the revolver should be raised and lowered thus…' intoned Albert Senior, chewing on the end of his cigar. He elaborately mimed the movement of the revolver for the benefit of his son,

'…allowing the revolver an immediate return to the firing position. Now come on lad, let's see what you can do.'

The garden at Sedgeley before them stretched away down to the tennis court and the canal beyond. It was rich and green and roses were planted everywhere. There were oak trees lined to the right of them and a few sycamores down the terraces to the left. The house was at the top of a hill, with the canal at the bottom and the garden flowed between the two. There were steps down the side and the lawn was cut into terraces which spread before the wide range of the Webley revolver

Albert reached gingerly for the thing, which felt big and heavy, in his hand. He thought at first, he might need two hands to hold it, but then he grasped the gleaming handle firmly and reached for the trigger. He had to stretch his fingers some way. He was standing as straight as he had watched his father stand and he raised his arm slowly, deliberately, but with a final flourish, just as he'd been shown. With one eye closed, he lined the muzzle of the gun directly on the target they had made. It was attached to a small wall built right at the end of the garden for this sole purpose. He squeezed and the gun burst echoed across the plains of the Trent, the bullet ripped into the target and bounced off the wall. He turned to his father and grinned a warm grin. Albert Senior glared back at him,

'Now go on Lad, I told you I'd left you three. That one was to the right, adjust your aim accordingly.'

18

Albert turned back and aimed to the left, the gun feeling more accustomed now. It nestled in his hand. This time the bullet missed the target completely, bouncing off the wall. He shot again immediately, aiming dead centre and gritting his teeth. His chest was knotted with the anticipation of it. This time he gasped as the revolver burst and saw the paper target tear further as the bullet hit the bulls eye, right next to where his father's first one had gone.

'That's better Lad, well done. Now next time, avoid over compensating with the second shot, always aim dead straight. Here are six, we'll take three each again and this time, hit the target every time.' He dropped the bullets into Albert's eagerly outstretched hand.

Inside the house two excited young faces, and one older, anxious one, watched the stout figure of the moustached man, in his shirt and braces, give the bullets to the little boy in his shorts. Harriet had known that Albert had wanted to initiate young Albert into his love of guns. She had visibly paled each time he had shown them to the boys. Each crack of gunfire made her jump slightly, and each made her grown inwardly. There would be no end to it now and Cyril would be next. Gunfire in the garden, the neighbours had mentioned it to her before and now there would be twice, then three times as much.

'How's he doing Mother?' Lois was thirteen, 'I bet he's a rotten shot.' She giggled. 'I saw it hit the target!' squeaked an excited Cyril, just seven. Harriet knelt down and draped their arms over both their shoulders.

'Now come away both of you. Guns aren't toys and it's time for tea.'

She hushed them through into the large front room with its big black furniture. The maid had laid the table with sandwiches, and scones heaped with jam and cream.

They had only had a maid for a year. Albert Senior was an ambitious man who had done so well for them. His Father was a plumber and Harriet's was a mechanic but Albert's successful estate agency had allowed them to move to the Park, Nottingham's elite district. He had been a city councillor for the Castle Ward in Nottingham for 6 years now and only this year had been appointed a Justice of the Peace. Harriet had to match his rise with one of her own socially, and she had worked hard to become good at the role of a wife to a successful and prosperous business man of high social standing, and a mother to his three children.

Now she poured tea from a white china teapot, and added sugar from a shiny silver spoon. The china cups sparkled and the linen was white. She served the children first making sure they ate their sandwiches, before they tucked into the scones. Then the boy known as 'Food Shifter number One' came running in the room and had to be told to go back and wash his hands first, then eat a sandwich and not just dive in for a scone.

'I hit the bull three times second time round Mother, then shot a stick before Father could hit it.' Albert chimed.

'Now Love, I've told you before, don't talk with your mouth full.' Harriet caressed the boy's shoulder lovingly and he smiled back at her. 'You're a good boy Albert'.

Albert Senior suddenly appeared and filled the room.

'The boy's a good shot, he's done well today. Three out of three second time round, chip off the old block, hey up Albert, you've had a good birthday today.'

The boy beamed brightly, and then a little later, brighter still, when the maid appeared with his birthday cake, lit up with nine bright burning candles.

Sunday March 25th 1917. London Colney aerodrome near Shenley, Hertfordshire. There were butterflies looping the loop in Flora's stomach, as Mr Piper drove the Austin Morris into the airfield. Mr Piper had talked so fondly and so often to her about the young airman who had billeted with him. Mr Piper was a close friend of Flora's father whom she had always known; at least it seemed that way to her. Her mother sat beside her in the car. Mother had read about Ball in the papers and 'any chap needed carefully checking for suitability, if he intended courting her daughter'. Anyway, she secretly had quite a desire to meet this 'knight of the sky', as the papers called him, in the flesh.

The airfield consisted of Nissen huts and stern hangars made from wood, and in some places, grey canvas with the blue, white and red cockade painted on them. This was the home of 56th Squadron, a squadron of handpicked flyers. It was the Royal Flying Corps' answer to the threat posed by Baron Richthoffen's flying circus, which was a legend that was just about to break. Air superiority always hung in the balance by a clouds breath in the skies above France.

Piper was humming to himself. He was the architect of this moment. It was his fifth attempt to thrust the energetic and charming enigma that was Flora, into the arms of the even greater enigma that was Albert. He had watched Flora grow and blossom into a woman of fine character with those deep, dark eyes. Young men were mad about her. She shone: a truly stunning beauty with a thick wave of deep, dark hair. Yet, there was something strong about that face, and a determination about the girl with the haunting tremolo voice. She was also doing her bit and Piper loved her for that too. Her only fault in Piper's eyes was that she drove like a strange female demon; he had only been in the car with her once, but had made a mental note never to do it again.

And then there was Albert with those deep, dark eyes. He hid his light under a bushel and was only content messing about with an engine. He was a good looking boy, with a red, ruddy face, under a thick wave of deep, dark hair. Yet, there was something so strong about that jaw, and a determination about the boy, who said so little. He was doing his bit, as far as Piper was concerned, far better than any man in England and Piper loved him for that too. Albert was a flyer, his element was the air. What he had done for his country was absolutely wonderful.

Piper was a man who had carried a secret for too long. He had discovered two people that were, quite simply, made to be together. The day he had realised it he had danced without music. It was a EUREKA! Moment, and once he had known it; the whole world had conspired to make it true; over and over again. The more contact he had had with each of them since that day, the more convinced he had become. It was as if they were brother and sister, born on the same day but from different parents.

But Piper was also a blunderer; and the journey here had been a long and difficult one. So many arranged meetings were cut short by wartime, and the speed things changed. There was the day he had driven Flora to Hendon, only to see the tail of the plane fly away. Then the time he had driven an embarrassed Albert away from St Albans, suddenly realising she was away at the farm. He had blamed himself for days after that. He had only one worry at this moment in time; that both of them fizzed with the same nervous energy, which might make the sparks fly between them, at this; finally-about-to-happen-Thank-the-Lord, meeting, and the two of them might not get on. He had told Albert he must talk to Flora and he had told Flora, how quiet and sensitive Albert could be. He had forgotten to tell Albert that Flora could be the same way too sometimes, but he knew he had done a good job of selling Albert to Flora, and Flora to Albert.

Piper had worked hard at this. He had not been subtle. He had quite simply badgered them both, beaten them both into a submission, if such a thing was ever possible with either of them. He had written, telephoned, telegrammed, driven, flown, walked mile after mile and then, written, telephoned, telegrammed all over again. He had said all the right things, at all the right times to all the right ears. He had encouraged, coaxed, manipulated and simply stated the fact to each of these two young people, that they were perfect for each other. There were some days since the moment he had realised, when this was the only truth that Piper knew.

Now he carried a precious cargo over the Hertfordshire countryside. He looked carefully across the aerodrome; there was Ball's plane and the boy standing beside it. Piper accelerated as much as he dared, towards the meeting that he had made them both long for.

3.

Monday May 7th 1917. Vert Galant Aerodrome.

France was so beautiful at this time of day. The land around the aerodrome had avoided the carnage-ridden, shell-pocked death that was twenty minutes flying time away. There was only the machinery and buildings of the Royal Flying Corps to show that this was war. The mechanics and riggers and technicians had started to rise, and the airfield was assuming its ordinary air of busy preparedness. The first

23

engine had spluttered into life, the first SE5, standing square faced and chocolate coloured in the East aerodrome.

Ball had designed the plans for the hot water pipe to come to his hut himself. Maxwell had known where there was a bath, left outside one of the farm buildings now converted to an office. It had easily been commandeered. The pipes had also been found, by one of the mechanics whom Ball had bought tobacco for on his last leave. A mechanic who even now, was waking with a hangover that Ball had provided. Ball lit the fire under the primus stove and began heating water for tea.

He shaved in the bowl, whilst the bath filled; his father would have said; 'Just stand in the wind and the fluff will blow away.' Then Ball used the dental powder, sent by his mother, to clean his teeth. It was gritty, but afterwards the mint flavour was welcome. His bath was almost cold, but that was how he liked it at this time of day. To get it hot took the stove two hours. He had become used to cold baths at Trent College. He could remember cold baths in the winter, when the drip froze on the tap, followed by a Cross-country run. He scrubbed away the oil and soot with the strong-smelling carbolic soap. Then he lounged in the water for just a minute and allowed himself a single glimpse of Flora once again, at Shenley on that first day. He had flushed the second he had seen her, Piper had not exaggerated at all. She was beautiful. He opened his eyes and sprang out of the water. The thick white towel was rough against his skin.

He put on his uniform, making a mental note that he should start by replacing the wood to the right of the hut. He still wore the lapel badges of his first regiment: The 2/7th Battalion, Robin Hoods; The Sherwood Foresters, or more correctly, Nottinghamshire and Derby Regiment. If he hadn't chosen to fly, he may have died

24

with them at Gommecourt, on the first day of the Somme. No other Officer of the RFC wore any badges other than those of their own regiment, but this was Ball.

A phone call to the adjutant confirmed the order of the day; his flight was to go on patrol from twelve thirty. He would need to work on the plane from eleven o clock. Unless the call came, from the sound of Archie – anti-aircraft fire bursting high in the sky- meaning a rare Hun sortie this way, he had time to work on the shack and plant the geraniums Lol had sent from home.

He was aware that the rules of the game had changed. His reputation was based on one aircraft shooting down another. Last year that had seemed easy, the hardest part was finding the Hun. Now they rose to the air in great red formations of fighters. Now there were thirty planes shooting and diving and wheeling and banking into the clouds. The French air seemed full of daggers.

Ball had his face to the ground, examining the soil, when Rhys-Davies appeared. 'Halloa Captain Ball, how are your marrows faring today Sir?' Lieutenant Arthur Percival Foley Rhys Davis was 19 years of age. The year before, he had been Captain of Eton, a boy with the whole world to look forward to. He had bright blue eyes and like most of the other pilots in Ball's squadron, he was well turned out. His uniform was smart, his dark hair combed and his cap was perched neatly at an angle.

'They're well Rhys, but I am afraid the soil was better at Savy. How's the back?' The Flight commander was wearing slippers, and looked more like a schoolboy than a pilot. On his first day in France, Rhys Davis had crashed his plane on landing and had not flown again for a time because of a sprained back. He had also needed a new plane.

'Oh it's fine now, I just felt such a fool.' Rhys Davis recoiled at the memory. He had let the plane bounce on landing. It had veered to the right and the wingtip had caught the ground, breaking off the wing.

'Can I get you some tea? I have been sent some top notch cake.' Ball smiled at the boy, this was one of those inexperienced pilots he had been sent here to encourage. The boy Ball, suddenly felt old, in truth, he had been feeling old for some weeks now. He had seen too much.

'Tea would be topping, thanks, and just a taste of your cake would be splendid, thank you.' Rhys shifted uneasily from one leg to the other, until Ball made him sit on some packing cases that were destined to become more of the shack. Ball registered his discomfort and tried to put him at ease. There was just a year between the two boys, but it was a year of combat flying and 43 aircraft fleeing, falling or exploding in the sky. It seemed a chasm to Rhys Davis at this moment.

'So Rhys is this a passing visit, or did you want to learn about gardening?'

Rhys Davis decided to be direct.

'I wanted to ask you Ball, about fighting. This is my first trip out here, as you know, and I just wanted to know where the best place to really smack them is. I just want to do my best really; not let anybody down.' He sipped the tea that Ball had made and ate his slither of cake from a tin plate.

Focussing on something in the distance, Ball talked softly, looking down at his garden:

'It's not the same now. It has changed. They are quicker than we are and they don't go out alone anymore. Last year it was easy some days. Just rove and you'd find one, a solitary two-seater or an albatross. Now they hunt in big packs. You have to get above and behind them, and then swoop down. Sometimes I let go with the Vickers just to scatter them. Then get under the straggler, the one who is slow to break off. Get close, so the others will be afraid to let you have it, in case they do him more damage instead. Then rake him underneath with your Lewis gun. Give him a drum or two, but keep one spare for the way home. As long as he doesn't fall on you, you should be able to watch him go down.' He paused to sip his tea, all the time focussing on the same spot. The younger man allowed the silence, out of respect and because of the cake. Ball continued:

'You know, the worst thing is when you see them go down in flames. I can't think of anything worse than that. To die like that…' He wrenched a weed from the soil and flung it to one side.

The silence was broken by the sound of the engine of a Spad taking off from the direction of the hangars. Rhys studied the face of this small quiet man who had come to mean so much to the squadron in its opening days, and then he too focused on the horizon.

'I was meant to be going up to Oxford this year. Instead of sitting amongst scholars discussing Plato, I find myself in a field in France asking someone the best way to kill a German; someone's father, husband or son. This war is so bloody beastly.'

The golden Spad flew over them, rising at fifty feet; a light mustard seed yellow bird with a beautiful red white and blue tail.

'True,' said Albert, looking high into the air, 'but at least you just might get to fly one of those, one day.'

Monday May 7th 1917, Hacketts Farm.

27

The farmhouse kitchen was a long low room with whitewashed walls. A clanking wooden door at one end led to the dairy, a room that was cold even on the hottest day of the summer. At the other end, the smell of bread baking dominated the room. Hackett had stood the loaf on its end like a tower, on the long brown table, around which three of the girls were seated. Hackett did not slice the freshly baked loaf; he carved it expertly.

It was Amy's turn to make the tea and she busied herself at the range which Hackett had lit whilst the girls still slept. Cleaning it was their least favourite task of all on the farm, but the bread was always good. This moment, before breakfast was made, was one of the few in the day when the girls could relax. Flora was reading the paper from the previous day, Violet was darning and Beatrice was knitting socks. Beatrice was always knitting socks. Since the need was made known for warm woollen socks for men in the trenches in winter, Beatrice had knitted hundreds of them. As 'Patriotic workers', the girls received eighteen shillings a week, twelve of which had to be paid back to Hackett for their keep. Beatrice hoarded what little she had left to buy wool. It was another running joke amongst the girls that Hackett needed to switch to sheep for Beatrice's wool collection.

They thought her a 'good egg' for doing her bit. They thought her motives were good. She could never tell them why she knitted, the debt she was trying to repay.

In 1914, when the war broke out she was just 17. She and Madge had gone to the music hall; they went whenever they could afford it. Their favourite theatre was the Empire in Leicester Square. Vesta Tilly was on, the male impersonator, the one who sang 'Burlington Bertie', but at that time, just as the war had started and everyone expected it be over by Christmas, all her songs were patriotic ones. She said 'God bless all the brave men in uniform' and everyone stood up and cheered them. She wore a top hat and a silver suit and a thick black moustache and just like a man, she asked the other men there, like she was one of them, 'When are you going to the war?' When she sang 'Rule Britannia' the crowd stood and roared. Some one once called Vesta 'England's best Recruiting Sergeant' and they weren't far wrong. She had two real recruiting sergeants, one either side of the stage. She sang 'Sorry to lose you, But we think you ought to go.' Then she walked down and through the audience and touching men on the shoulder, and when she did, they'd go and sign up, there and then. Oh, it had been grand.

As they left the Theatre, Madge pointed out a poster on the wall where they waited for the bus. It said:

TO THE YOUNG WOMEN OF LONDON. Is your **best boy** wearing Khaki? If not, don't **YOU THINK** he should be? If he does not think that you and your country are worth fighting for- do you think he is **WORTHY** of you?

Neither Madge nor Beatrice had got a best boy at that time, but it really got them thinking. It had been Beatrice's idea; they would join the Order of the White Feather. In August 1914, Admiral Charles Fitzgerald had called upon women to give white feathers to men who had not joined the army. This was what they had proceeded to do. Beatrice kept a set of feathers in a cigarette case; she had got them from a cushion. It was like a game at first, all the girls were doing it. They'd choose a spot and whenever they saw a young man not in uniform, walk up to him with a smile and present it like a gift. At first they would then hurry off, but later they would call out as they went:

'Get yourself off to the war!' The fun was in the reaction of the victim. Some turned and argued with them or tried to explain why they were at home. Others, who had received enough feathers by now to make their own fan ignored them, threw them back at the girls or let them fall to the floor. There was one night they'd left the Old Kent Road swirling with feathers.

Then there was the boy. He was such a handsome lad, tall and green eyed. It was Beatrice that handed it to him; they had taken it in turns. She should have run back to Maggie then, but something in his face made her do it and then stand still, Madge thought she'd forgotten to run off. He looked down at her then at the feather and closed his fist on it. He'd looked Beatrice straight in the eye and said:
'But I'm only fifteen Miss...' She opened her mouth to say something but then Madge had pulled her away. Her last view of him was standing under the gaslight looking forlorn and lost.

But she had seen him again after that. She was sure it was him. He was on Page three of the 'Evening Standard'. That was where they put the casualty lists. It would say YESTERDAYS CASUALTIES 321 Officers and 2438 men. Underneath the lists of all the London men killed there'd be two pictures. Beatrice had often wondered how they chose the two out of the two thousand. Was there some race of shame as soon as you received the telegram to get your son's dead face in the paper? One day it was him. It said: Private Thomas Sutton, 17, Royal Fusiliers. Died of wounds. He still looked too young for his uniform, he was still good looking and he was dead. Beatrice had begun knitting.

She put her knitting down now while Amy served the tea.

4.

Sunday 21st October 1906 Nottingham Canal

'I've got one!' Thrale's heart was beating fast. The reel spun, pulling line out as the fish tried to escape. Thrale let the line run, and watched the float plough beneath the water. Albert ran up clutching the landing net. Cyril and Holmes ran behind him across the towpath.

'Reel him in Bob, but make sure you give him plenty of slack line.' Albert was breathless and flushed. All four boys gathered round to watch Thrale's fight. He could feel the fish pulling away from him to the right, so he pulled the cane of the rod to the left, pointed it down at the water and began to reel in.

As the fish's head broke through the waves, Thrale could see it was a silver-green pike with a long thin head. Pike had razor sharp teeth and were born killers, the best fish in the canal. The boys had ridden from Sedgeley down to the bridge at the Marina and then along the towpath to the lock after the bridge on Peveril Street. The

31

wash from the lock stirred the bottom of the canal dredging up food for small fish, which in turn became fodder for pike. They fished at the point in Castle lock where the water runs white.

'It's a pike Bob, and a decent one at that.' Albert slipped the net under the fish as he had done many times before for his father. They hauled it on to the gravel towpath. Thrale held the long thin mean killer of a fish proudly, while Albert retrieved his box camera from the saddle bag of his bicycle. He took a picture of a grinning Thrale, holding a grinning fish. Then Ball held the long green killer in his arms.

'I'd say a pound, or maybe two Bob. Let's put her back.' He handed the fish to Thrale who held it for a second under the water before watching it slip away and into the dark and murky green.

Albert had brought his Scout patrol fishing for the day. He was leader of the red patrol of the First Lenton Boy Scouts that met in a shop on Willoughby Street every Tuesday night. There, led by Mr Robert Norris, they would march and sing and kneel down in circles. They followed the ideal of Baden-Powell, the hero of Mafeking. They wore smart green uniforms, and made fires to mash tea on. They studied knots and ropes and made things from wood.

The canal was a favourite spot for Albert. He loved the way the water seemed to ooze calmness on to the towpaths. He could sit here for hours watching the tiny red float move slowly downstream, waiting for the elusive killer pike. The canal at the bottom of the garden was a good place to catch roach and bream, but it did get busy with narrow boats; one of which was passing now. The canal was an artery for Nottingham's industry.

A white swan with a haughty red bill bobbed across the waterway. Albert watched as it began a take off, its broad wings suddenly looming out from under it and its webbed feet trailing through the surface, leaving a wake through the water. Its powerful wings battered the air. It took off and flew along the canal bank rising to swoop over a bridge.

Suddenly, Albert grew bored and restless. The engine problem had been ticking over in his mind all day. He called to the raiders and they packed their rods away. Tackle was bundled into saddlebags and the rods were dismembered, wrapped and then tied to the cross bars of their bicycles with string. Then Ball's Texas Raiders pedalled furiously along the towpath. They split into two separate flights to navigate their way around a plodding carthorse, pulling a gliding narrow boat through the water; then rejoined again as a single squadron to file out on to the road and across the wide tree lined Castle Boulevard.

Albert decided to take them the long route back and doubled his efforts to pick up speed. They went under the great yellow sandstone rock that was Nottingham Castle and swooped through Brewhouse yard. The journey was harder now, the pavement went uphill and as they rounded the Old Trip to Jerusalem pub, Albert's legs began to feel the pace of the cycling. Castle Road was busy with Lace workers out on their lunch breaks and clerks from various offices going into town. Although the day was warm, the workers wore heavy Edwardian clothes. The women had blouses buttoned high up to the neck with white puffy sleeves and wide brimmed hats. Their skirts reached down to their laced up boots. The men wore suits and overcoats and hats. Each pedestrian was a potential obstacle to the boys. The raiders began their slower ascent of the hill, avoiding the pedestrians coming out of doorways. At last they reached the entrance to the Castle and turned left down the hill.

Now it was Holmes' turn to be lead rider. His bike went quicker downhill than the others. He rang his bell gleefully as he began the long descent down Lenton Road. The wind whipped through them as they darted down the tree lined pavement. On their left, the Castle Rock stood for centuries. In front of them were the hope of empty pavements, downhill freewheeling and the promise of tea. Holmes' bike bumped over the pavement. He missed his footing in the pedal, and wobbled dangerously, before regaining control. The other rangers were not slow to see their opportunity. Even little Cyril managed to get past him as they raced down the hill.

Holmes viewed the way back with some anxiety. He was enjoying the ride but he found tea at the Balls quite hard. The last time, they had soup and he picked up the bowl like his father did. The other boys had laughed. Mrs Ball was kind but he still felt so silly. His bike picked up speed again; he crossed the road and rolled down the pavement on the other side. This was to be his undoing; an elderly couple and their dog were suddenly in front of him. His bike skid to a sideways halt as the others swept him aside.

Finally the road began an upwards incline and the boys, tired now, slowed to a gentler pace. There was a final uphill rise when Holmes caught back up with them, then they rolled into the drive at Sedgeley house in formation, with Albert in front.

Before tea, Albert took them to his shed. He showed them the latest engine that he and Cyril had found. It was now in many pieces which they had been lovingly restoring; cleaning, polishing and coaxing back to life. Much of the weekend had been spent on three pieces of brass that would not fit together. The frustration of it hurt even now, they had tried it over and over again and they would not fit. There were three rings that should rotate together, but all the boys had were three bits of round brass that stubbornly refused to fit.

He allowed them the briefest glimpse of his radio. He was so proud of it. His Father had said that he might be the first boy in England to own such a fine thing. Just the night before, after he and Cyril had finished digging up worms to use as bait; he had deciphered signals in Morse code that came from Spain. He had spent many hours attaching the aerial, high up under the eaves of the house. His Mother had worried so to see him up there, but he had enjoyed the view. From the top of the house you could follow the canal's drift right down to the Trent.

Then the Raiders were in action again out on the lawn. Thrale and Holmes formed a raiding party to attack the Alamo, which was the Balls' shed. They circled some time before attempting to attack the door. 'Cill' and Albert stood furtively either side of the door, their stick guns at the ready. When the ambush came, all four boys ended up wrestling on the shed's wooden floor. Naturally as leader, it was Albert who fought his way to the top of the pile, and then led them all in for tea.

Mrs Ball had baked a Victoria Sponge cake, Albert's favourite and he eyed it with anticipation. First there were sprats to eat and sweet sugary lemonade. For Holmes, whose family lived in less luxurious circumstances than this, in a terraced house in Willoughby Street, tea at the Balls was an extra special treat. Mrs Ball knew what the boys were like, boys meant mess. She used the cheaper cutlery and darker tablecloth, but this was still a feast. Albert Senior was away, looking at a plot of land he hoped to buy and then sell for 'a tidy sum'.

The conversation turned to football. Thrale had been to see Forest play the day before. They had beaten Clapton Orient in a game which became exciting in the second half, after Clapton had had two players sent off. Bob was describing the second half with increasing ardour. Standing on a box in the Trent End, Thrale had watched Arthur Grenville-Morris, Forest's best ever player, score twice in a 4-0 Forest victory.

Even before the Bob had got to half time, Albert's mind had drifted from the conversation. Despite the lure of the cake, he had thought of something. He asked to be allowed to get down from the table, Harriet was surprised he had asked before the cake but she agreed, as there was an unspoken urgency in his request. He strolled purposefully back out into the garden and towards the shed. He could hear Thrale's voice rising in tone as he described to Cill and Holmes a particularly exciting part of the game, but he did not take in any of the words.

The shed was silent and smelt of timber, a deep woody creosote smell. This was his den and his workshop, the place where he was happiest. In the cool stillness he found the three brass rings just where he had left them. Then he searched for and located a steel rod, the thing he had thought of at the tea table. Diligently, he offered up each piece to the next, searching for the solution. Sure enough when he placed the rod through the brass pieces and inverted the second one, it worked. His small neat hands moved carefully, quickly and with intensity. He tried the thing again, the rings rotated superbly. The rod was covered with a thin black oil and looking down at his palms Albert realised he'd have to wash them again if he was to get any of that cake. He placed the engine parts back neatly on the bench and returned to his friends.

Back at the table, Harriet surveyed the excited boys. She was so proud of the way Albert led them. He was such an intense little boy. It was very unlike him to ask to leave the table before the cake. She loved the boy deeply; watching him grow had given her such pleasure. There was a fierce loyalty between them which Albert Senior found hard to understand sometimes. Later, when she looked back, Harriet saw these days as a wonderful spring, before the deep sad winter of the war.

This was how the heart of England's boyhood would be stolen between 1914 and 1918. This and this.

Saturday July 1st 1916 Gommecourt, the Somme, France.

Almost bent double by the weight of the pack on his back, Holmes hobbled forward in the darkness, continually keeping one eye on the man in front. Progress was slow, the support trenches were crowded, and the communications trenches were full. They had left the village of Fonquevillers, or 'Funky Villas' as the tommies called it, hours before. The scale of the preparations had been immense. They had been watching it for weeks with trepidation. The first signs, while they were training had been the arrival of the guns; thousands of them, dragged by horses and mules and men all the way along the line.

Then five days ago, the barrage had begun. Day after day, night after night, the guns blasted and pounded away. All day long the earth had seemed to waver, and not be a solid thing. When the earth beneath your feet cannot be trusted, when the sun and moon are blotted out; when smoke is your only horizon, fear runs through you like your blood. Every night the sky was aflame, the air burst and the fires consumed it. The whole world became a massive firework display. The anger was incessant,

37

the flames were ever present. Yet somehow, this became normal. Now the guns had ceased and it was eerie. It gave Arthur the spooks.

The Robin Hoods had begun this same slow journey to the trench that they had dug two nights before, but the 'big push' had been postponed. They had slumped back to Funky Villas the next morning. There was relief because they were alive and disbelief, because they would have to do it again. Ammunition stocks were now being preserved for the next day's effort. Arthur had become so accustomed to the barrage that when it stopped, a rising panic began somewhere deep down inside of him. As he limped forward now, through thick muddy trenches that were lined with men weighed down with heavy packs, and far, far heavier fears; he knew the worst part stretched before them with the threat of the morning's sunrise.

They had dug their own jump-off trench thirty yards in front of the British front line. It had cost them many lives. The sappers and engineers had begun the digging, but when the Robin Hoods were judged to have sufficient cover, they had been sent out to complete the job, crawling 30 yards across no-mans land with a shovel in the dark. The Huns knew they were there and the shells burst around them and above them as they dug. Several men had been killed as they worked. Arthur had lost Pals.

They had been a fine bunch of lads, ready for anything, when they had first assembled in the Drill hall on Derby Road. Then they were sent to Luton and Harpenden for training. Ball had been with them then. Then he flew away and they went to France. They had manned the trenches at Ypres, in a particularly difficult stretch of the line. Ypres was a salient; the Huns surrounded them on three sides. There they stood in rat infested holes being picked off by artillery barrages and snipers; Whizz-bangs clattering the air around them. Then they had heard that they would be moving to the Somme, for the big push.

As they had left the village that afternoon, they had trooped past the Regimental Sergeant- Major, one of the fiercest in the army, or so they thought. This rough barking man was standing silently, weeping and unable to speak. It had begun an anxious hush among them that continued and intensified the nearer they got to the front. Now it was palpable, it was etched in the faces of every man.

In front of him the man stumbled but Arthur couldn't help; he was carrying a pack which weighed eighty pounds, a rifle and three bags of trench bombs. The man righted himself slowly, the whole sad procession halted. He turned back to Holmes. 'Blast this mud, we must be almost there by now'. It was Thrale, now Corporal Thrale, and Battalion Medical Orderly. He had somehow managed to adapt himself to army life better than Holmes. For Holmes, it had become a daily trudge, his only efforts were to ensure his own survival, but Thrale had taken to it all with relish and gusto. He had formed the battalion football team with another Corporal, a former Notts County player. They had done well, until three days ago, when they lost four-nil to a team of enormous Scotch lads, some of whom had played professionally before the war.

Thrale had gained a scholarship to Nottingham High School, and had used the rudimentary Science they had taught him there, as a means to further medical training. As the M.O., he had made it his business to know all the men. Not just those who had been there from the start, but the new blood too; the frightened little boys that were crawling forwards now behind and in front of them. He knew their medical histories, their dysentery, their coughs and their lice.

He looked at Holmes, a German shell burst somewhere in front of them, probably over the new jump-off trench they were making their way towards. It briefly illuminated Holmes face and he saw, the fear and resignation there. Thrale was twenty, Holmes just 19, yet they moved forward slowly with faces marked with all the death that they had seen. The war had made them old.

Thrale reached the point where they began the crawl to the trench. He hesitated as he stood on the firestep. Captain Leman was there, encouraging the lads to go forward. He smiled when he saw Thrale:

'Over you go, Bob and when you get there, keep an eye on the younger ones for me will you. Everybody's a bit jumpy tonight.'

Thrale nodded. 'Will do Sir, there'll be fine. How's the leg?' Leman had needed help from Thrale's First Aid kit the week before when they were training for the push. 'It's fine now Corporal thanks to your help.' The two men nodded, and then Thrale began his crawl. The ground was covered with a thick oozing mud that clung to every shred of your uniform and equipment. Thrale pulled himself forwards with his elbows at first, then when he had moved a little way from the line he began crawling on his knees. When no shells fell around him and no machine guns spurted fire at him, he rose to his feet and struggled forward through the mud, in the dark, following the slouched figure in front of him. The mud was over his ankles and his feet seemed to be so heavy, each step was pure effort. The mud groped up at him and held onto his uniform. It slithered over him and refused to let go. He was exhausted when he finally fell into the trench.

The trench was worse than 'No Man's Land'. It was crowded with boys trying to clean mud from their tunics, their packs and their rifles. The muddy water in the bottom of the trench here rose above Thrale's knees. It was all he could do to find a space in line and sit, leaning his tired head against the wall. Holmes lined up next to him, tired and drained. It was almost three in the morning. It had taken twelve hours to get here.

The boy on his left was 'Nutty' or Maurice Nutt. He slept with his head against the side of the trench. On his right, Holmes took his pack off and stood it on the fire step. He retrieved a pencil stub and some paper and began to write the letter. Thrale followed his example. It was hard to see so his writing, normally small, neat and precise was full of vague loops and sometimes wandered almost off the page, but he wrote.

Dear Mum and Dad.

I hope you are both well. I love you and miss you both. Give my love to Connie and tell her I am thinking of her.

We are ready for the big push now and go over soon. I want you to know that I have tried my best for you and done everything I can out here to make you proud. The Captain says that things might be tricky, so if I don't make it, at least you know I have done my bit.

Thank you for everything you have given up for me. I appreciate the sacrifices you have made. I love you both and will always be, your son.

Bob.

At 4 am, there came the first hint of dawn, and rain began to fall. A few of the men had fallen asleep or dozed briefly. Then the Captain arrived and made his way down the trench. He announced that zero hour was to be seven thirty. Arthur glanced at Bob with shocked eyes and open mouth, and Bob instinctively knew what he meant.

41

They'd be going in daylight. They'd be going up against the German guns without night's cloak to hide them.

The petrol cans of hot coffee laced with lots of thick treacly rum arrived ten minutes later. As they shared a can of the strange vaguely petrol tasting liquid, which was wonderfully warming; Bob could see how Arthur's hands were shaking. He talked to him about football, Forest's progress in the Midland Section of the War league. Most of the men had lost interest since the war began, but Thrale had clung on to this as some semblance of normality in a world which had clearly gone mad.

Gradually Arthur felt better, even if it was the rum. For him, the waiting was worst of all; it felt like he had been standing there forever, up to his thighs in mud, waiting to do the thing he had learnt you never did at Ypres; soon he would raise his head above the parapet. Soon he would walk into the guns.

At five o clock, an eternity later, the barrage began again. This was the firestorm that would kill the last remaining Huns and shred any remaining barbed wire that had managed to withstand the last five days pounding. Now they were right in the middle of it. The German artillery responded, which surprised Arthur, he'd been told their guns had been put out days ago. As they stood up to their knees in the mud, itching from the lice and so, so tired; the skies above them seemed full of steel and lead. The earth shook beneath them in spasms. There was no opportunity to speak, the noise made your ear drums hurt. It was as if the world was ending. Fire spurted above and around them; the air was thick with fumes. Every so often, a shell would smash into the earth nearby, and they were showered with tiny pieces of steel and earth. One cut into Arthur's right hand and he stood detached, watching the blood flow. He became aware that his hand was shaking and his teeth chattering.

They stood there, as the world exploded angrily around them. Their only comfort was the thought that no one on the opposing side could possibly have survived this. For much of the time, Arthur was alone as Bob tended to minor wounds, caused by the shelling. For Bob, the time passed quickly; he was busy, dealing with shrapnel wounds and splinters. One of the boys was fortunate enough to get a 'Blighty' wound, which saw him pulled off through the mud in a stretcher, back to England before the attack began.

Arthur's attention was drawn to the rifle at his side. This was the way he'd be in control again, after so long of mere obeying. He had the power to choose where the bullet, the one he knew would inevitably come, entered his body. No one would realise in all this madness, that he had done it himself. He picked up his rifle, pointed it towards his foot, then realised he could not. In anger he raised it at the sky, and in despair, he pulled the trigger. The rifle clicked lamely in his hand. Nutty who had watched him, laughed a drunken laugh. Arthur pulled the wooden thing to him; it was cold and wet against his face. He was showered with earth and bits of metal again. He reached for the cloth in his pack and began to clean his weapon, quickly, desperately then frantically. Nutty, became aware that his rifle was wet too, and the two of them cleaned and cleaned, trying to get the things dry again.

At Seven twenty, the guns raised their desperate cry to a crescendo and then there was an earthquake or so it seemed. The first mine had been blown up further down the line. The ground shook again at 7.28 when the rest of the mines blew parts of the German line high into the sky. Then, at Seven twenty nine, there was complete silence. There was not even a bird in the sky. There was no sound at all, the world was suddenly empty. Nutty next to them began singing. He had enjoyed the rum too much. Arthur's heart was beating as loudly as a drum. He was visibly shaking, all of him shook now. To keep himself going he had been praying fervently. He begged Jesus to spare his life, he asked God to stop this horror. Nothing happened.

They could not speak to each other in that final silent minute. They shared everything through each others eyes. Bob reached out a hand and Arthur, weeping now, shook it. The smoke shells landed in no mans land to provide cover. Then they heard the sound of a bugle call from the German lines.

Deep in his dugout, thirty feet below the earth Leutnant der Reserve Metzner of the 9th Battalion of the German 91st Reserve Infantry had told the bugler to sound in readiness. Everywhere his men were busy. The barrage had initially taken them by surprise, in this normally quiet section of the front, but it soon became all too obvious that an attack was planned. They had waited deep under the earth for the barrage to subside. For days they had felt the full force of the guns and many good men had died. Now his Observers had seen troop movements. It was time to take revenge for the horror; his men were deafened, tired and almost blinded. He ran up the steps from his dugout to the little Z trench and checked personally that each of his gunners were ready. Then the smoke screen descended. He exhorted each gunner to fire, as accurately as he could into the smoke, at anything that moved. He ran from one machine gun to another, making sure all the ground was covered.

In slow motion, Captain Leman called 'Fix bayonets, Come on the Robin Hoods' and blew the whistle. The first wave, 'A' company mounted the firestep as one and began walking in a line into the smoke. The Captain rose from the trench and walked calmly and precisely towards the death that awaited him. Arthur could not move, his legs had gone, but Bob reached out a hand and pulled him over the top. They walked

44

the first few steps into the smoke through the mud towards the wire together. Shells exploded around them. The first thing Thrale noticed on his walk was a shell, a dud, lying unexploded in the earth. Then he saw another and another and another. The things had not worked; the barrage had not done its job. They continued their serene walk, struggling under their packs through the killing ground. Suddenly, Bob had to jump to one side, banging into Arthur to avoid Nutt who had exploded into pieces of flesh, bone and blood when a shell hit him. It might have been a British shell. Thrale's left side was wet with Nutt's blood.

A breeze caught the smoke and blew it further down the lines and the Robin Hoods lost their cloak of invisibility. All along the line, men began doing funny little dances as the machine guns tore into them, arms flailing around, spinning and falling into the earth. There were men screaming and shouting for stretcher bearers. Men were crumpling down into the soil; soil running with blood. You could smell the blood and hear the low groans of men dying everywhere. Someone further down the line had managed to set off a red flare, the signal to the British guns that the troops had got this far, it was also the signal the Huns used to bring down covering fire. The first German shell extinguished the flare; the next cut the boys up into pieces.

The rattle of the machine guns grew louder and louder. Arthur and Bob carried on walking towards the wire. They could see no gap, no way of getting through it. For a moment, they were lost. A moment was all it took. The first bullet shattered Arthur's wrist and passed right through it. Bob looked at the useless hand hanging off the end of Arthur's arm, and began to reach for a dressing. Arthur, the pain contorting his face, threw off his pack with his good hand as the second bullet went into his thigh.

45

He slumped onto one leg in agony. He was grunting and dribbling, his head sagged forward and his helmet fell off.

Bob knelt down and put his arms around his friend. It was all he could think to do, Arthur's pain was unbearable. The next bullet blew away part of Bob's shoulder and then two tore through his chest. Then the machine gunner lingered and the bullets showered them, fingered them, entering their bodies in so many different ways.

The two boys were sitting cuddled in the mud. Their blood mixed together and dripped into the soil. There was no movement now. They stayed there for the whole day. A bored German machine gunner used Arthur's head for practice while waiting for the next wave and shot it right off, but the two boys still knelt there, cuddling in the mud.

That night a British shell found them by chance and they were never seen again. No one ever told them that they had died in a Diversionary attack and not the main one. No one could tell them that the preparations at Gommecourt had been designed to let the Germans know an attack was coming, to force them to commit their reserves. If they were successful, it would have been a bonus, but it was just a diversion. It did not really matter. 600 men of the Robin Hoods were slaughtered in a Goose Fair sideshow. The Generals had predicted casualties of ten percent, their maths was poor again, and eighty percent of the Robin Hoods joined the earth that day. It was the worst ever day in the long black history of British warfare. In just an hour or two of miscalculated madness, Nottingham had lost all her finest, purest sons.

5.

Sunday March 25th 1917. London Colney aerodrome, Near Shenley, Hertfordshire.

Piper stopped the car and applied the handbrake. Then he went round to open the door for Flora. His hands were trembling with excitement as he helped her down. He led the way towards the aeroplane and two figures strolled over to meet him. There was a tall man and a short man. The taller man was tidy and smart. The shorter man had a creased tunic, scruffy looking flying boots and a shock of black hair. Flora knew at once that this was Ball.

The pilots came over to meet her, she shook Jack Leach's hand and then the boy was before her. She meant to shake his hand but just held it. She was vaguely aware of the streak of oil across his forehead, but to look at that she would have to look away from his eyes. They were deep and dark and pulled her.

Piper grinned. 'Flora, this is Captain Albert Ball. Albert, may I present Miss Flora Young.'

What did he say then? She remembered it until she died.

'Topping' he said and smiled. His face was flushed. His eyes were so intent on her, she almost blushed. She smiled too and there was something born then. Something remote, yet permanent; something forever.

'Delighted to meet you at last, Miss Young.' He sheepishly let go of her hand and was for a moment, at a loss what to say next. There was a pause. Then he tried hard; 'Fancy a flip?' He waved his hand in the direction of the Avro two-seater that he and Jack had been preparing for her. Flora was wearing a pale yellow dress which seemed to dance in the faint breeze. Her hat was yellow too, and underneath it were coils and coils of tawny brown hair. Albert liked looking at her; he enjoyed her face; her dark eyes and distinctive jaw line. She was a beauty and he was smitten with her.

47

She had a little bit of the look of Tec about her. Tec was Albert's first proper girlfriend; they had held hands together over a period of three months last year. Albert's father had finally suggested that the relationship be ended and the boy had acquiesced. The boy had told her that he could not fly into a fight as bravely with her loving him, as it was like flying with an observer, you were responsible for two lives, not just your own. Tec had agreed entirely with his father's decision.

In a bustle and a pain, Flora's Mother arrived beside them. She looked at the aircraft as if it was some strange prehistoric beast. Her frown spurred Flora on immediately.

'That would be splendid' she heard herself saying.

The plane was a long thin thing with very broad wings. There was a red, white and blue cockade painted halfway down it.

Jack was despatched to find flying gear whilst Albert and Flora stood there, not quite knowing what to say. There was an eternal pause between them it seemed. Ball smiled and coughed. He shook hands with Mrs Young, who glared at him. He struggled to explain to her that the plane was quite safe and Flora would be fine.

Jack came back with a big brown leather coat and flying gloves. Flora put them on. She felt vaguely ridiculous in the enormous coat. The plane seemed flimsy; it was made of linen, stretched over a wooden frame. Only the paint made it brittle. They found a step ladder to help her into the Observer's seat. She placed one foot upon the wing, and reached up accepting Albert's arm, and then she lowered herself down in front of him. She had never flown before and suddenly everything was happening in slow motion, everything happened monumentally.

There was a big black machine gun right in front of her, she turned to him.

'Do you want me to use this?' He grinned a boyish grin and winked at her:
'Only if we see a Hun and I think that's quite unlikely over St Albans.'

The mechanics that had been surrounding the aircraft moved to the front of the
plane. They linked arms to improve momentum, and to make sure the prop man was
pulled away from the scything propeller. They spun the propeller, which at first just
spat and banged back at them. Then they tried again and this time the big wooden
bird sang.

Once the engine was warm, Ball called 'Chocks away' quite routinely. The men
pulled the triangular chocks from under the plane's wheels away and it started
moving. It bumped and wobbled across the field. The mechanics walked with them
at the wingtips.

Flora saw her Mother's scowling face flash by and then was aware of the bounce of
the plane. She looked determinedly ahead of her. It was a strange feeling to be at the
front, as if the boy was pushing her forwards. She looked forward, to something new.
She felt every bump and pebble in the field and then the wheels lifted, and the bird
flew. She had to close her eyes as the machine pulled from the earth, rose from the
ground. When she couldn't look down, she concentrated on the propeller spinning in
front of her. Below her, the fields of Hertfordshire became brown and green squares
on a patchwork quilt. The roads stretched out like scars across the countryside,
everything turned to toys. Then they were bursting through clouds and the sky was
rich. Flora had never known anything as beautiful as this.

They rose steadily, he flew so gently for her, and he did not want her to be afraid.
She was more than he had imagined. He had seen her yellow dress fluttering and
dancing on the breeze and known immediately that she was a part of his air. He had

49

seen her coy smile and her gentle glances. He so wanted her to think well of him. He would have done things to impress her: the Avro would easily loop or roll, but more than anything he was frightened; he did not want to worry her, he simply could not scare her away.

Flora was growing used to the sky and its wonderful forever. The engine had at first seemed loud and insistent, but now it seemed to her that it purred. She loved the way that the propeller sang. She loved the way you could see it and not see it. She was starting to think she might love him too. Albert was shouting and pointing, but she had no idea what he was saying. The engine noise drowned him and he was lost from her. She turned to see him, he smiled back at her and she just loved him, right then and there. Then the plane swooped low as he pointed, and she felt a sweet mixture of exhilaration and fear. Below her, when she had the courage to look, was St Albans, laid out like some giant plan. She had never seen it this way before. She could make out the model village market place, her house and her church. Now it was her turn to point and shout:

'That's our house,' she turned round to him and Albert raised his thumb. He dropped the plane down low over the market place and then lifted her up, over the church steeple. He banked the Avro 504 to the right and pulled it up towards Radlett to take Flora back to the field. She had time now to smile and laugh. Flying felt good, although some of Ball's turns lifted your tummy into your mouth. You felt every current in the air, you rode every wind. She allowed herself another look back at him, those dark eyes, that dark mane of hair. He seemed so at ease as he guided the machine through the air. He was so at home up here in this vast empty blue. His world was somehow upside-down, his streets were all in the air. His home was up here, where the tiny figures below might see him, but never be able to touch. Up here, he was Lord. She had been so right to fly with him, she'd never have understood otherwise. He flew the fragile thing, the wooden linen thing, gently for her and in wide circling turns. He courted her on the currents of the air.

The bird began descending in a gentle spiral and she saw the aerodrome, the car, her Mother: that other world.

Monday May 7th 1917. Sedgeley House.

Albert Ball Senior awoke at 7 precisely, stretched and went to deal with his ablutions. He washed whilst singing a hymn;

'When a knight won his spurs in the stories of old,

He was gentle and brave and gallant and bold'

He began to wax his moustache, which was difficult to do while singing so he was forced to hum, sing and mumble:

'With a shield on his arm and a lance in his hand,'

The waxing complete, he applied a little pomade to what was left of his hair whilst reaching a crescendo:

'For God and for Valour he rode through the Land.'

He dressed quickly, struggled with his braces, and became rather annoyed at the stain on his tie, but soon found another. This was to be an important day. He had sold the land at Beeston and today contracts would be signed. Albert so enjoyed the days when his killer instinct was proved right and another deal was done; and done for a tidy sum. He found his tooth powder and began methodically scrubbing his big white teeth.

He marched downstairs and kissed Harriet Good Morning, His tea; toast and eggs arrived instantly. In fact, the tea was under the cosy before he spread his napkin and sat down. The post arrived; there were many business letters and one from the boy. He wrote Received and the date on each with the pen he had placed above his plate for just such a purpose. He checked each business letter briefly and added a note on each envelope as to the necessary action involved. He did all this whilst munching his toast, attacking his hard-boiled egg and drinking his tea.

Then he wiped his hands on the napkin and stood with his back to the window, the room darkened as he carefully opened the boy's letter with his silver letter opener. This was a familiar routine, he had carefully read every letter the boy had ever sent; even from school, had then acted upon them (and saved all the letters, in case of future importance). He gently took out the flimsy sheet of paper. At the top was the familiar blue crest of the RFC. He hadn't wanted Albert to fly, but the boy was determined, and once determined, unchangeable. It was only twenty years earlier that the idea of anyone taking to the air in anything other than a balloon or airship was unthinkable. His boy it seemed was a born-flyer, a real asset to his country, in this the war that would end all wars. Being the Father of a hero had done his own reputation and business interests no harm at all.

The boy's letter was written in his usual hard-to-decipher hand. His spelling had always been eclectic at best. He wrote late at night after a hard day's fighting and his words sprawled across the page.

52

Alderman Ball JP's heart beat faster as he read the letter. The boy's tally had gone up again; he'd been getting two almost every single day. He beamed as he read of the topping fight his son had won. He was in front of the Frenchman now, the highest scoring allied pilot! Marvellous, this was the news his Father had been waiting to hear. The boy had done him proud.

'Harriet,' he called out. 'Harriet, he's done it!' His wife entered the room silently; her face was stoic, resigned to it all.

'He's got 38 now, best score of all the allies. The boy's done well again.' Harriet winced; they would lose him for sure. So many young boys were falling from the air and at the front. She wanted him home again .She looked at her husband who was puffing out his chest proudly and lighting a cigar to celebrate.

'Then he's done enough', she said, 'let's hope they send him home now; I want him safe Albert, back here with his family.' The pain was almost too much to bear; her fears were welling up inside her. She busied herself abstractedly with the breakfast table.

'They'll let him come home now Harriet, the boy's done it. The figures are there. Highest scoring allied pilot in the war; the boy's a marvel.' He felt such a mixture of pride and anticipation.

Alderman Ball's mind raced over the matter then he reached for the telephone. He dialled the familiar number and was straight through to the Editor of the Nottingham Evening Post. The boy was a hero; the people of Nottingham needed to know that Alderman Ball's son was a hero, hey up, the biggest hero of the war.

6.

Monday May 7th 1917 Vert Galant Airfield.

The boy had wished a fond 'Cheer O', to the even younger boy, Rhys Davis, who had an early-morning patrol scheduled for 8.30. With the unusual luxury of time on his side, Albert strolled to the farmhouse and the Officer's Mess there, for breakfast.

The Mess was a long low room that used to be the parlour of the farmhouse. It was popular and quickly became crowded. It had white walls and black beams. The atmosphere was warm and welcoming, not as stuffy as other squadron messes. In the other squadrons he had served in, he had avoided the Mess, he found conversation difficult sometimes, but the 56th was full of his friends. He was the first pilot chosen for this squadron and Blomfield had allowed him a say in choosing the best pilots around. He had chosen his friends.

He was almost the last to arrive. The rest of 'A' flight were sitting round a small wooden table. The Mess staff were busying themselves around the room, bringing eggs, toast and tea to the Officers. Someone in the regiment had had the sense to keep the hens at the farm laying, and the boys now enjoyed their eggs as a result. He had been greeted continually as he made his way to the Mess, sometimes, just sometimes, he felt like the squadron mascot. These were normally old goats, and that was exactly how he was feeling now, like an old tired goat with a headache. Bessie, their own mascot had made a fine meal of part of his garden, just a week ago.

It was funny that they stayed in their flights, even at breakfast. The drunk they had had a few weeks before, had been the start of that. The rest of the pilots were drinking shampoos, a lethal mixture of champagne and cognac. Albert was sober, but high on life and took full part in the debacle that followed. Blomfield had called for Soda siphons and the Mess staff duly delivered. The squadron split into its three flights and battle commenced. Siphons squirted from every angle. A quarter of an hour later, the whole Mess was awash. The boy had succeeded in destroying B flight with a spiralling attack they had not been expecting. They were drunk, their reactions were slow.

Albert had carried Lewis home that morning, from a mess awash with rivers of soda water, and from men hardly able to stand but in fine and noble spirits. Lewis was the squadron philosopher, he was deep. The boy liked him a lot, after all, he was just another boy. The boy Lewis seemed to have the power to articulate all that the boy Ball, felt but could not say.

Ball sat down next to Maxwell and the mess staff immediately fussed over him. He drank the tea and ate the toast. The eggs arrived later. By then, he had become aware that 'C' flight were around the table directly behind him. Lewis was directly behind Ball's back. He was a year older than Ball but you would never have guessed that. A boiled egg was placed in front of him. He asked for the salt and received it; then he salted his egg. He was still talking about the causes of the Lewis gun jamming to 'Duke' Meintjes, and forgot where he was sprinkling his salt. A mound formed on the tablecloth. Lewis took a pinch of salt between his finger and his thumb. He threw the salt over his shoulder; it was the only thing to do. Ball, sitting directly behind Lewis, back to back, heard the salt grains bounce off the grubby shoulder of his tunic. His dark eyes darted around all the men in his flight, there was an unspoken agreement between them then.

'Oh, Sorry Ball, I had no idea...' said Lewis.

'You will be,' said the boy. 'Oh yes, you will be. 'A' flight at the ready, defend your leader!' he shouted now, and his flight stood.

55

Ball reached for the salt cellar and prepared for the counter-attack. Maxwell reached for his eggshell with a grin. He aimed to escalate the conflict quickly, drawing 'C' flight into a fight that they could not possibly win. He crushed the eggshell in his palm and launched it heavenwards towards Melville; the man he considered to be 'C' flight's weakest link. Then 'A' flight swooped in a synchronised attack; Maxwell had gone for the whole pepper pot and directed it at Lewis. Ball followed up with a bombing raid of salt, using his fork as an escorting scout.

'B' flight, quiet until now, rose to the challenge. The orderly atmosphere in the Mess dissipated and was replaced with laughter and mirth. There was a taciturn understanding between all the boys, this was a fight and the best flight would win. The air was suddenly filled with salt, pepper then egg shells, shouting and laughter. The respective flight commanders assembled their flights, whilst grimly clinging to their pieces of toast as the battle raged.

Albert was pouring the contents of his table's salt cellar over the back of Lewis's head when the short gruff figure of Blomfield, the C.O. marched into the room at the eleventh hour, and all hostilities ceased. Blomfield pretended not to see the mess his pilots had made of the Mess. Such ragging was good for morale. Albert ceased hostilities and withdrew his artillery, also known as a salt pot, as did all the men. Battle was over, at least for the moment. Lewis was relieved, but made a mental note that he owed Ball one. The conflict was 'to be continued'. All the combatants were suitably deferential towards their Commanding Officer. They laid down their condiments and the grains were at last silent.

Monday May 7th 1917, Hacketts Farm.

The girls marched in their wet hob nailed boots to the lower field. Hackett led them, and then showed them where to dig. They were surrounded by verdant green trees. There was not the comfort of animal warmth here, just thistles and a ditch. There was no glamour in this; and these were young girls who would have liked glamour. This was a ditch that they had to dig. The earth was black and thick despite its dryness. They had shovels and they began digging. Amy scattered the soil too close to the hole, Beatrice dug and dug. Violet became violent in her efforts to master the brambles and the soil. Flora dug deeper and deeper. There was silence but for the grunts and the sighs of the tired girls; that and the sound of the spades cutting into the soil.

Long slender white hands wore blistered palms. The day bore down on them and Flora became tired then displaced. In her own mind, she rehearsed letters to the local, then the National press. She had reached the point of no return, in her last letter to the boy; she had begun begging him to come home. She intended to wage a war of her own. She could not bear the risks that he was taking, fighting every day. He had done enough now. She could feel Violet's pain and Hackett's sorrow tangibly. She had no desire to join them. He must come back. She would make him come back.

At first, she had decided he was just a good looking boy. Then, when she flew with him, there was something else; a kingship. He wrote to her all the time and she had hidden her feelings for so long. Her last letter was a shout, a cry of disbelief, a plea; that he would please, please come back to her now, whilst he still could. She had seen him fall to earth and break, so many times, in her dreams. The flimsy, crude wooden and linen things just broke all around him, like the wings of a butterfly, snapped off mercilessly by some wretched boy. She did not want to end up the same way as almost all the women she knew; grieving some loss. He must come back.

He had surprised her from the start. She had never expected him to fall in love with her the way he did, like a wounded aircraft falling from the sky. Oh, she wanted him home, she needed him home, she loved him whole and wanted to keep that.

The overwhelming smell in the lower field was that of manure. Hackett had felt such a mixture of emotions when he first brought the young girls here. The field needed draining, but it did not sit right with him asking young women to dig. The trees here were old and gnarled. Some bent into the wind, like Boer War veterans leaning on sticks. The field was good for cabbages and Brussels sprouts but needed draining first; and at this time, the order had gone out that all agricultural work must be done by hand, to preserve fuel. They were digging a ditch, and then afterwards he would make them chop down trees; a man's job, Hackett knew.

But knowing and living were poles apart Hackett had found, and so the girls dug. He got alongside Amy, his favourite girl and began digging with them. Beatrice was highly strung, he had found. Violet always seemed angry, Flora was haughty, he struggled to connect with her, although he admired her most of all, she had undeniable beauty. Amy was easy. She was warm and laughed at all of his jokes. She was pretty, yet robust. She was undaunted by him, most of the time and he liked that. Sometimes, he thought, he might as well have been flying one of these new aeroplanes. His world was upside down. Slender girls were digging drainage ditches and his sons were dying one by one, whilst he still worked the land; just like his father and generations before him, stretching back on this one piece of land, to a time when the soldiers wore shiny silver armour, and went on more realistic crusades.

They had taken his horses in 1914, when the world first went mad. The soldiers had come to the village and taken all the horses, everybody had lost. They had led them away tied together with rope and the village had watched their friends and servants disappear forever. It was a terrible day.

He had three beautiful animals. Bess was a black carthorse with the thickest, heaviest, shaggiest hooves. She had pulled his father's plough. Now she was ploughed into the soil in Belgium. Plover was a donkey with a heart of gold, he had cried when she went. Her guts had been strewn across the trenches at Gallipoli when she was being dragged up to the front to carry water. After a week, her rotting carcass had provided regiments from New Zealand with a smell that would never leave them.

Lupin was a young grey colt with breeding potential. He was the leading horse in the long roped line. During the retreat from Mons, the Queen's Lancers had come under an artillery barrage, Hackett did not know how many men had died and would never know that his beloved colt had sunk to its knees there, before his intestines were blown out of him. He would never know which parts of Lupin, the advancing German troops, cut off from their supply lines, had cut from his body and eaten, first charred in their fires and then later, in desperation, raw.

There were men in the trenches that could sleep soundly all night, surrounded by a variety of rats and lice and displaced human limbs, but who still were broken hearted to see noble horses fall and roll in pain; whinnying and screaming out their final haunted breaths in situations they were not to blame for, and would never understand. Beautiful horses with huge shell holes in them, majestic horses with broken bleeding necks, noble white horses turned into a bloody red stew. Men that died in battle, had known the risks and could die nobly, quietly, with dignity. The hundreds of

59

thousands of horses killed had no understanding of the reasons for their pain. They knew only blind terror. The site of a wounded mare with a shattered leg still dragging her dead mate, dead driver and destroyed cart along the floor whilst screaming, could still break the heart of the toughest battle scarred veteran.

Hackett missed his horses like he missed his sons, but he knew, he would never see any of them again. He had begun to pretend his last remaining sons had gone as well. Each telegram had taken a piece of him, and two more would mean there was nothing left of him. So, he prepared his mind for more sorrow by writing off what was left. He did not look forward and did not look back. Each day without death now was a blessing, but he felt prepared if more bad news came. This war was a great harvest and all the crops were all dead ones.

Flora stood up to her ankles in the water. It began to rain and she tugged her oilskin coat around her. She lunged her foot onto the ridge of the spade and it cut deep into the soil. Then she made a swooping movement with her arms that brought thick clods with it. She overturned the soil then lunged again. Her spade hit something solid. She scraped the top of the blade across it, it was too big to be a stone, and it sounded like wood. She called out,
'Amy, what's this?' Amy came running over and the two knelt down and looked into the hole. Amy started scraping the soil off the thing, it was a wooden box.
'You've found buried treasure,' Amy laughed. Together the two of them clawed away the soil around the box and lifted it out onto the surface. It was a small wooden box, about a foot square. Scraping further soil off the top, they saw thick black writing in a childish hand. 'Secrets' it said.

The two girls looked at each other. 'What can it be?' said Flora, 'Why would anyone leave such a thing here?'

'Let's open it and find out' said Amy with a smile. She felt around the lid to find the hinges then opened the box. Gradually they began to see it had been packed with a child's things. There was an old horseshoe, with the word 'Lupin' painted on it in white. There were three lead soldiers, one missing an arm. There was a pack of playing cards, which looked well used. There was a clump of black horse hair tied with a parcel tag; the brown tag said simply, 'Bess'. There was a shiny glass marble and two brown conkers, both stringed. Finally there was a piece of greying parchment. Amy unrolled it and they read together: the childish scrawl.

'propety of tony hackett hacketts farm wood end hertfordshire if found please return'.

'What have you found there?' Hackett looked down at the box in disbelief. Gradually he realised what each piece was, then he silently gathered it all up and turned his back on them. He walked back to the farmhouse, clutching the box and shedding tears he did not want the girls to see. They watched his back disappear across the field and saw how his shoulders sagged.

He went to the barn and slowly turned over each object in turn, each rich with memories of children and animals now gone. He stroked the toy soldiers and the marble with his thick thumb. He remembered Tony by the fire playing with the soldiers, the fight that broke out when Jack had cheated at cards, the proposed conker tournament that could now never happen. Well, Tony was gone; hit by a sniper at Loos, Jack had gone down with his ship. It was the horse's hair that finally did it. It broke him and he sobbed. He threw the box at the Barn wall and it shattered. The contents climbed the wall then fell into a heap. It was all useless to him now, a world he could not forget, but never be a part of again. Alone, he walked back to the wood, the women and their work.

7.

Monday May 29th 1916 Savy Aubigny aerodrome, near Arras, France.

Harper finished pouring the oil into the compact little green flying machine that was the Nieuport 16 scout, and put down the fuel can. He wiped his hands with a rag while looking over her. She was primed and ready; of all the planes he had worked on, this was the one he liked the best. Her lines were straight, her wings strong. Three of them could move her round the airfield easily and the engine was easy to get at and pliable, they knew it well now. He was particularly proud of the fact that the curved gun rail for the Lewis gun above the cockpit, which enabled a flyer to pull it down and choose his angle of attack, had first been designed by men he knew.

Captain Cooper and Sergeant Foster, both from the 11th had made the first one in the Workshop lorry. John had had the second one.

He glanced over to the gently bellowing Bell tent from which the new boy was emerging. Someone had nicknamed him John. He had forgotten the first line of the joke, but it must have been a good one because the new boy was just called John by every member of Number 11 Squadron. It was an improvement on his previous nickname, when they first arrived they called him 'One lonely testicle.'

Harper and Lewis had been Rigger and Fitter of Lieutenant Wright's plane up until he had been shot down two weeks ago. Wright had survived but his Observer; Captain Gerald Blunt Lucas had been killed. Lucas was a proper gentleman of the very best kind, and it had been a sad day when he went. Harper and Lewis were bequeathed to the new boy, Ball also known as John. John had been upset by the loss of Lucas; they shared an earnest eagerness for the job. Lucas was older than Ball and came from India. He was eager to do his bit and John talked to him because of that, John did not talk to everyone. Lucas was so eager; he'd climb on a wing at 10,000 feet to protect a damaged plane. John was so eager; he slept at the aerodrome to be within earshot of his machine. Lucas could draw Albert out of John, something the rest of the squadron had failed to do. John had come highly recommended, having come from flying a Bristol scout with 13th Squadron who shared Savy Aubigny aerodrome.

11th Squadron only had two of the new French designed Nieuports and John was now something of an expert in flying scouts. The boy was rarely out of the air, looking for fights behind enemy lines. Some days Harper and Lewis had been woken by him at 3am, wanting the plane ready. On several occasions he had not come down until after 10 at night. You had to admire his commitment. He was always so desperate for a fight.

John strolled over to them, when would someone up top speak to him about his uniform, Harper wondered. The youngster was such a scruffy lad. The C.O. had been a stickler for discipline in the past, yet this John got away with anything. He flew without goggles or mask to get a better view he reckoned. Harper wondered how he avoided getting French insects in his face and his eyes.

'Morning Harper, Morning Lewis, how's she looking this morning?' John stroked the side of the big green bird.

'Very good Sir, all ready to go up when you are,' they exchanged a salute and the boy bounced into the cockpit. That was how the boy was different; Lucas and the rest would have chatted for a few minutes first, asked about their wives or something. John just wanted to be up and off. He had this hunger for it, this need.

John checked each gauge in turn then began to call out the sequence. Harper and Lewis took position at the prop, Smith was on the tail. Ball loved this plane, it could out-climb the Bristol easily, and he thought it could out-climb every plane the Huns could put against it. It was light and small and fast. He was so proud of it; there were only two chaps in the whole of the RFC that could fly one of these.

He had been in France for months now; leave had been cancelled three times. Only his love for the plane and his time in the garden stopped him feeling really poo poo about it all. There had been days when he had been going to bed at six in the evening, he felt so fagged. He was getting his share of the action which was great but it was tough at times too. The French plane would certainly make him feel better. When he flew her, she felt like the best aircraft in the skies.

64

He began the sequence.

'Switches off, petrol on.'

'Switches off, petrol on,' called out Harper in reply, and then, 'Petrol off.'

Harper and Lewis revolved the long slender prop two or three times and stood back.

Albert made adjustments then called 'Contact'.

'Contact' was Harper's repeated call, then he and Lewis carefully spun the prop and the engine kicked in. The Nieuport hummed to herself on the lush green aerodrome. Albert checked all the dials again while she whirred and then with a salute to Harper and Lewis, now standing at either wingtip, he shouted 'Chocks away'. The wooden blocks were pulled from under her and she began moving forward into the breeze. She picked up speed quickly as she roared away and soon she was lifting off and beginning her climb. He banked her towards Arras and then sat back whilst she lifted him up into his air. He took the usual piece of cake out of the pocket of his flying coat and began to enjoy the panorama of the blue.

It was lemon cake, good cake made for good flying and this bright morning, it had just turned 8 O Clock, the air was wide and fine. He was going fishing and he felt so sure today he would get a bite or two. He had fitted the plane with a small circular convex mirror to command a clear view of the whole sky. He had learnt the trick of his eyes being everywhere when he flew. Now where were those big fish feeding today, he wondered and glanced up and down the twisted shattered countryside 10,000 feet below him.

He had worked so hard to get into a single-seater. They had made him fly the cumbersome BE2s for a long time. The Germans called them 'flying pianos' and they were no match for the Fokker, but the Nieuport was the Fokker's equal. He hated flying two seaters, you could not take a risk unless you were willing to risk someone else's life as well, and he never was. He had had to be persistent to get flights in the Bristol with Number 13 squadron, and finally transferred. Major Hubbard had told him when he first arrived with the 11th, that they followed the simple ethos of Lionel Rees, a Military Cross winner with 11 kills so far. His philosophy was a straightforward one; get in the air, and find a Hun, then attack. How this suited Ball. He did it every day the wind allowed him.

His eyes struck a dot in the mirror and he began to turn right. The dot became bigger and he turned and looked through slatted eyes. It was a big German carp, a two-seater, if he was not mistaken, a Roland or a LVG. As he got closer he could see the cream colouring and the black crosses on the wings. He readied the Lewis gun, pulling it down the black curved rails. The Roland was 4000 feet below him when he began his dive. The speed gauge flickered half way between 100 and 110 mph. His chest was gripped with the anticipation of it, his face was red, and he couldn't breathe as he came upon it, closer and closer. He could see the two men now, in helmets, and the observer was busy taking a photograph.

A photograph, a seemingly innocent thing; but it was a photograph that would be given to the German artillery; a photograph showing the English boys hiding in their trenches; a snapshot that could be used to kill.

He gritted his teeth; she was just 30 yards away. His finger hit the trigger and his bullets spat into her; tearing away at the thing. He could see the sudden panic, the Observer going for his machine gun. He could hear them shouting to another. He held course and fired and fired, the plane in front of him suddenly banked away. He felt sure he'd got the pilot. He'd only fired half a drum of ammunition and then he saw the great cream fish with its fish's tail, fall vertically out of his sky. He watched it go down but did not see it hit the ground.

He breathed again and smiled; his eyes still everywhere. He began to hum loudly, his Victory song, a melody from Schubert's Unfinished that he liked to play on the fiddle. Now he hummed it in stirring fashion, for his guns had made sweet music. He returned the Lewis gun to its higher position and began to search again. He'd spent so many hours searching; the hardest part of fishing was locating the exact location, the stream in which the fat Hun carp took photos of the British lines below.

He cruised for half an hour; he had begun contemplating his usual trick of circling over a Hun aerodrome to draw them out; when once again; a dot came into the blue mirror, then another and a third. He banked her towards them, she was so light, this lovely French machine. He had soon learned to dance with her. The three planes were heading towards the shattered ruins of Arras; it was another big carp, escorted by two Fokkers. These were nasty little blighters, like baby pike with sharp teeth and he decided to wait a while. He climbed up behind and above them, back to 10,000 feet. He would bide his time. Gradually, another two planes appeared, coming from the right of him, between him and the other three. They fell in above them and for a time, he just stalked the five of them, unseen behind the sun's morning brightness. The escorts continued their way towards Arras and the carp swam off alone in a different direction above the ruins of Oppy. He followed it for just a little while before pulling down the Lewis again.

The heart began to beat quicker and the face became flushed, he felt his chest tighten as he began his swoop of death. He began spitting at them with his gun from fifty yards away, but this time his ammunition drum ran out before the Huns did. He banked away, now this was the tricky part. Ball steadied his plane out of range; he released a catch and pulled the gun right down. He grasped the empty drum firmly to release it. The thing sprung at him and he pushed it firmly down in the rack then quickly loaded the new drum. Then he forced the gun, and it was heavy, back into place. He used his shoulder to heave the black metal gun up the curved mounting until it locked. At last he could return his attentions to the scrap.

He turned on them again, bearing down on them with gun firing away in a deep bass voice, tearing away at them. The Observer was ready for him this time, and stood in his seat to fire back. Albert could see his determined face, his black moustache as they traded bullets. Albert was surfing the air currents, banking first one way then the other as he shot, and the carp struggled in the water with the hook tearing into its mouth. Then the cream thing fell away. He had felt the Hun bullets hit the Nieuport, more than half a dozen times, one had been pretty close, just behind his back. He'd tensed as the bullet had bounced behind him. He watched the plane's forced landing from high above then turned back to Savy.

He began to pray now, openly and out loud, thanking his heavenly Father for the protection He had given that day to the poorest of His sons. He thanked God from high above the clouds, feeling so close to Him.

He must have been over the lines when Archie started bursting around him. One shell exploded close enough to wobble his plane, then one hit. The plane bumped and bounced then levelled. Albert looked back and pulled the stick to climb out of range. He'd been flying too straight, making it easy for them. His tail had been partially shot away. Still he could see the fires bursting around him. He coaxed the delicate little thing all the way along the roads back to Savy, and landed it perfectly, without a bump. Excitedly, he told Harper and Lewis about his morning's victories whilst they looked at the bullet holes and tutted, and scratched their chins over the broken tail section. Then he bounded into Insall's Office, the adjutant, to report his double of the day. For Ball this was the difficult bit; doing the thing was fine, but finding the words to explain what he had done was hard.

Sunday March 25th 1917 London Colney aerodrome.

In the years that followed she had so often looked back on that day to try and find what had happened then, how the shy little chap had stolen her heart away. She remembered a series of pictures, brief moments they had snatched from fate. She remembered him helping her out of the plane, she was still exhilarated by the flight, the way he had courted her up there. He was smiling and he held out a hand for her and guided her from the cockpit on to the wing and then to the ground. He had held her hand for just a second longer than he needed to and she had liked that. He said so little, it was as if you had to coax words from him.

  While he reported some detail of the Avro's performance to the blue overalled mechanics, she had stood there, feeling vaguely ridiculous in the big leather flying coat, then he had turned and helped her off with it. The mechanics had pulled the plane away between them and taken it to a hangar, as if they were leading some enormous cow off to its milk shed.

'How did you like your flight?' he had asked her, and she told him it was wonderful to see the town from the sky, a place she had known all her life was suddenly different from up there. He had smiled proudly then, as if he had shown her some great secret.

69

Piper brought Mother to them and Mother was relieved to see Flora back in one piece. Piper had asked about his new plane and he walked them to the hangar to see it. He had been working on it for two weeks and he described to Piper the modifications he had made, but this was quite lost on her. There were two planes in the wooden hangar and Ball's seemed to have pieces of it lying around everywhere. It was as if he had a need to take it to pieces then put it all back together again before he could fly it. He had helped her into the cockpit and showed her the levers and the dials. Their heads bent low together as he showed her the pedals for the rudder. Then he helped her out, holding her hand for a fraction too long again.

Mother was beginning to be charmed by him.

'You really must meet William, Captain Ball, Flora's brother, he is fascinated by aeroplanes. Perhaps you'll join us one day in St Albans for tea?' She smiled at him and seemed less foreboding.

'That would be topping.' He said, looking sideways at Flora. 'I could come tomorrow, if that would be convenient.'

Mrs Young looked at the boy, she hadn't expected him to be so forthright, but she knew that in these troubled days, sometimes things had to move more quickly than one might want.

'Yes,' said Mrs Young, 'You can come tomorrow evening. I'll bake a cake. Flora will drive over and pick you up, won't you dear.'

'Yes,' said Flora softly, 'I'll come for you.'

'I'll be ready,' he smiled a wide smile and she smiled back at him.

'Tea?' chirped in Piper, 'now there's a thought'.

Albert suggested they walk over the bridle paths to the village and he and Flora led Piper and her Mother. The day was warm, the evening just beginning to settle in and he took her arm while they walked. The bridle path was lined with horse chestnut trees and a solitary squirrel crossed in front of them and went running up the bark of a tree. They watched the bushy red tail disappear among the foliage. He asked about William and told her about his people back in Nottingham. They came to a cherry blossom tree and he pulled down a sprig of pink blossom and placed it in the button hole of her jacket. He told her the pink blossom looked fine against her yellow dress. She had allowed herself the luxury of looking straight into those eyes then. He had flushed and for a moment there was a silence between them. She felt uncomfortable with it and found herself filling it with talk of the farm and her work.

This interested him. It appealed to his sense of everyone pulling together and doing their bit. He could not imagine her milking a cow, or digging a ditch. His arm seemed to pull her a little closer to him. His voice was hushed now. The sun was setting behind the aerodrome and the village was in front of them. The sky had a pink edge to it.

'Shepherd's delight,' he said and looked at her again. 'It has been so nice meeting you Miss Young.' She blushed. 'I do like the way you pile your hair up under your hat and it just Bobs there. Bobs, now there's a good name. I think I'll call you Bobs Miss Young and you must call me Albert.'

He took them to the little chapel first. He had been to Communion there that morning. It was a small white building, the stone above the door said: 'Holiness becometh thy House, Oh Lord.' Inside there were 7 or 8 pews leading up to an altar rail, an organ and a large wooden cross on the wall. It was small and intimate and warm, just like he was to her.

  Mother warmed to him even more now, this man of faith. She prepared the menu for tea the next night in her head as they walked down to the Black Cock pub, it did not normally open on a Sunday but Piper knew the Landlady and she fussed over him. They were brought tea and scones and sat in the lounge. Piper asked the boy about returning to France. He said they might go any day. Flora felt uncomfortable with this, she hadn't considered what it might mean to her before, but now it meant a lot.

  Mother poured herself a second cup.

'You know Captain Ball, our Flora has a fine singing voice, and she was classically trained, so maybe tomorrow we can entertain you for a while.'

'Splendid,' said the boy, 'I'll bring my violin. I have been teaching myself to play it and can make a tolerable noise with it now. Do you play Miss Young?'

'Oh no,' she replied looking again into those eyes, 'Mother plays the piano and I sing, making a tolerable noise like you I hope.'

  He laughed, 'Oh much more than that, I am sure.'

  The boy insisted paying for the tea and they walked back the way they had come. They talked about music, and he became much more animated. He liked Bach, but loved Schubert best of all.

Then figures strolled out in front of them. Two friends of his were walking from the airfield to the village. He introduced the tall figure of Cecil Lewis and the younger Rhys Davis. They were barely suppressing their laughter to see him escorting a lady.

  'Cheer O! Nice day for it Ball,' said Lewis.

'Cheer O Lewis, Yes, I'm sure' replied Ball, 'whatever it might be. May I present Miss Young? Miss Young, this is Lieutenant Rhys-Davies and the very dignified Captain Lewis.'

'Delighted to meet you,' Flora's hand was warmly shaken by each of them. Rhys Davis was dark and boyishly good looking; Lewis had a thin face and swept back hair.

'Delighted to meet you, Miss Young. You'd better watch our Captain Ball; he's a bit of a rogue on the quiet; or a very quiet rogue.'' Lewis grinned.

'They seem nice fellows' she remarked, after they had gone.

'Yes, they are both topping chaps, all the squadron are, but I'll take some ribbing in the Mess tomorrow. We have lots of laughs here'.

The evening was clawing in the darkness as they made their way back to the aerodrome and the car. They were silent, but it was less uncomfortable now, she did not feel the need to fill the space between them with small talk anymore. She did not want to let go of his arm, she had only just found him and the future was flying distantly above them like some dreaded zeppelin. They stood around the car in the dusk. It was agreed Flora would be there for him with her car at 5 the next day. He shook her Mother's hand and bade Piper a fond farewell.

They stood in the airfield together. He looked at her, silhouetted against his sky. There was so much kindness in her eyes and so much character in her face. The green field beneath them seemed to spin. She saw the boy before her. He seemed younger than her and there was something about him, some part she could not trace. Even now, at this beginning, this something between them, there was something lost.

Something she could never hope to find. There was intensity, a welling, and loneliness. He sort of leaked an air of loneliness somehow.

He let go of her arm and held out his hand.

'I look forward to seeing you tomorrow.' He said as he held her hand there. 'And to hearing you sing, Cheer O!'

'Yes,' she said, 'I'll look forward to hearing you play. Goodbye Captain Ball, it was very nice meeting you.' She let go of his hand and he, ever mindful of her, opened the car door and saluted, there was nothing military about his movement, she returned the salute, broke into a smile, and climbed into the car. Piper, by now in a state of sublime contentment, drove off and Ball was gone; although his shadow still covered her.

That night, she lay alone in her room looking up at the window. The sky was black and the candle beside the bed guttered as if caught in some unseen wind. Nothing had happened and yet everything. He was invading her thoughts constantly and soon would invade her dreams as well.

Albert lay in his billet; he was trying to sleep on the floor of a Nissen hut with five other officers from the squadron. Whilst they snored soundly on, he picked a pencil from his bag and scribbled a note to her by candlelight. He wrote:

Just cannot sleep without first sending you a line for the topping day I have had with you. I am simply full of joy to have met you.

He wanted to say so much more, but felt that this was enough. He soon slept soundly, deep under the spell of her.

The next time they met, he was covered from head to foot in black engine oil. And she was covered in cowshit.

74

8.

Sunday May 7th 1911 Nottingham Canal

Albert heard the weir before he could see it. All that falling water made a terrific
noise. You could hear the full force of it, its destructive power, and this was not lost
on him. He punted the Ark carefully, keeping as close as he could to the left bank. If
he drifted to the right, the Ark would be pulled over the weir, and he wasn't sure
she'd stay in one piece if she did. He punted her from the right side so she could not
drift the wrong way. He steered carefully as the noise of the rushing water grew and
grew. Finally he pulled her round into the lock and queued up behind the smoking
chimney of a narrow boat full of coal that was waiting there to take its cargo to the
hungry lace and hosiery factories in Nottingham, which lay before them.

The Lock was just about the half way point in his journey. He checked the silver
pocket watch he kept in his jacket pocket. It was a quarter to twelve, it had taken an
hour and three quarters so far, he was making good time. He was hot and the jacket
of his uniform now lay in the boat, his collar was undone and his tie hung loose.

He and Cill had been at Trent College for over a year now. He preferred it to the
High school as he found so much to do there. He was in the Officer Training Corps
and regularly patrolled and drilled with them. He also took a keen interest in the
bridge building projects; the summer before they spanned the Trent with a wonderful
200 feet construction. Now he was navigating it in a boat he had built himself.

The Ark, as she was known, had been a fine achievement. They had spent hours in
the Library planning it and it had taken a month to procure the wood. Albert had
wanted to do it with minimum costs, so they had used wood which had been left or

75

abandoned from all over Long Eaton. The thicker planks he could plane curves into, for the bottom of the Ark, he'd actually spent a few pennies on. The rest they'd begged and found. She was a grand little boat, painted white and with a seat constructed from two smoothly planed planks of pine. Albert punted her using a long smooth pole which had once been someone's clothes prop.

His first voyage in her was the one he had planned when he and Cyril had first been driven along the drive of Trent College by their Father. It looked a grand and stately place. The boys wore high starched collars and black ties. The Masters wore gowns and commanded immediate respect. There were twenty boys in F dormitory. The part Albert liked best of all was that Cyril also slept in his dorm. The two boys were inseparable at Trent and formed their own mutual support group. Albert was the one who came up with the ideas but Cill was his willing accomplice. He had wanted to come on the journey home, but Albert felt that the boat would be better with just one occupant for its maiden voyage.

He had harboured ideas about breaking a bottle of champagne over her side that morning, but he was too careful for that and for a fifteen year old, finding champagne was a bit of a chore. Cyril and the other two boys from the dorm who had carried her through the streets of Long Eaton, and saw Albert off from the Navigation Inn had broken the top off a bottle of ginger beer on her instead. The thirsty boys all then enjoyed the ginger beer, a satisfying compromise.

He was looking forward most of all to seeing his Mother. Parents weren't allowed at Trent, other than for Sports days or special occasions, and he had missed her so much. He had heard Cyril crying himself to sleep at night when they first got there. It was partly the shock of Trent with its first bell at 6.25, the cold baths, the cold dormitories, the cold classrooms, the cold other boys and the cold Masters. It was an austere place and they missed home so much at first. Once they had got used to it all, he had begun to love it. They had made lots of friends with other boys interested in the things they liked, or rather the things Albert liked and Cill followed; taking photographs, making things and building engines.

Albert's entire life was spent building, planning, creating, making and mending. He could not bear days with nothing to do, that was a private hell for him and at Trent there was always something to do. The school also kept you pretty fit, you did a lot of Cross Country and Albert did not mind that, even in the snow. He wasn't particularly good at sports, team games were not really his thing. He loved the workshops with the long lines of tools, carefully sharpened and ready to use. He also loved the armoury, the small squat building that stood at the side of the school. In the big curved arch round the door, there were carved Nelson's words from Trafalgar. 'England expects every man to do his duty.' Cill had taken his photo beneath it.

Building the boat had been a labour of love. You had to get each part just right, the pieces had to fit neatly together, so the joints had been carefully, sawn, planed, sanded then painted. His woodwork teacher had helped with the tricky bits. They had machined the big piece of wood that would form the bows of the boat together, but most of the work had been carefully done by hand. The others in the little group of boys that spent all their time in the workshops, had all taken a hand in the construction at some point, but always under the guidance of the master boat builder himself. He knew one day his mother would see it and he wanted her to be proud. He also knew that later it might be turned to profit, taking some of the wealthier boys for pleasure trips on the river, so it had to look the part.

He paid the lock keeper a halfpenny for his passage, once the water levels had been corrected, and continued on his way. This section of his journey was calmer; he was on the Beeston canal now, which flowed slower than the Trent. The landscape was becoming more industrial with factories, as well as the houses of Beeston Rylands. The traffic on the canal was different too. The narrow boats were piloted by men in flat caps with serious lined faces and love for their great pounding horses. It was relatively quiet today, it was Sunday and he had to avoid the lines of a lot of the anglers on the bank. Most of the coal travelled to the factories by rail these days, but there was still money to be made on the canal.

When he had first started out, all the river boats he saw coming through Trent lock were pleasure boats packed full of church outings, men in boaters and blazers and women all in their best long frocks. Her had paused and waved at each one in turn, the occupants wondering about the lonely boy punting down the river.

On his right, the playing fields stretched across Clifton Grove to the banks of the Trent. In the distance he could see the University, sitting proudly atop of a hill. He had worked out from a map in the College library that there were seven bridges between here and home and he began counting them off. He reminded himself that when he got home he was to pack some fishing gear into the boat so he and Cill could go after pike in the Trent at Long Eaton, when the fishing season started next month.

The Ark was not the first boat he had constructed. The raft he had made the summer before in Skegness and the subsequent attempts to rescue it, once it had floated away, had become a part of the Ball family folklore. As usual in each one of their stories about Albert, there was a point in it when he had almost died. The almost-drowned story was a welcome change to the story about him setting fire to his Nursery at the age of five, and almost burning alive. Today he had been most careful not to add to that oral anthology of tales of risks he had taken.

Harriet was at the kitchen window. She had prepared the beans for their dinner and was scraping the carrots, when she saw him enter the garden by the gate at the bottom, behind the tennis court. She called Albert Senior immediately:

'Why Albert, come quickly, it's our boy'. She ran down the garden to meet him and he stood with his arms stretched wide. Albert Senior loomed behind her,

'Hello son, by it's grand to see you, however did you get here.'

The boy, still enwrapped round his doting mother, beamed at him.

'I sailed a boat which I built with Cill at College.' Lol came out of the house to see him and there were more hugs before the admiring family trooped down the garden terraces to the canal, where the ark was now tethered.

'Why Albert, that's a fine boat. The boy's done well hasn't he Harriet?' Ball Senior positively clucked and cooed over the handiwork of his sons. Harriet was so pleased to see him there, coming all this way to see her. He was growing into such a wonderful young man.

Before setting out on the long voyage back, Albert ate roast beef and Yorkshire pudding, in the warm and smart surroundings of the front room at Sedgeley. The boat lay lower in the water, as it slipped through the waters of the Beeston canal that evening. The ark was brimming full with the cakes and fondant fancies, the marzipan fruits and the chocolates, the tinned peaches and the biscuits that Mrs Harriet Ball had instructed were to be shipped out straight via the canal, to her best boys.

Monday 26th March 1917 St Albans

Albert watched Mrs Young's back as she began the introduction to the song, perched at the piano in the long drawing room. The men, Albert, William and Flora's father were sitting on deep brown sofas. The women were in front of them at the piano. Flora sang:

'Thank God for a garden, be it ever so strong

Thank God for the sunshine, that comes flooding it on,

Thank God for the flowers for the rains at the dew,

Thank God for the summer that brings me you.'

My, she had such a fine voice. The hackles on his neck had risen with the first line and when she sang that last line she looked straight at him. His heart danced and he was unsure whether to laugh or weep. He had to bite his lip for the whole of the second verse.

'Thank God for the sunrise, for the new morning bright,

Thank God for the sunset that is shepherds' delight.

Thank God for the cornfields, for the moonlight of blue,

Thank God for summer, thank god for you.'

She had risen to a beautiful falsetto crescendo and then brought it all down and back to him, by delivering the last line straight to him with her eyes. He and Will and her Father burst into applause at the end of the song. He shouted 'Bravo', what a splendid girl she was. What an absolutely top-notch girl.

Her father seemed a quiet sort. He was an architect and surveyor who had designed the rather fine townhouse that they lived in, right in the centre of the marketplace. Her mother was artistic; she had ideas of becoming a sculptress before the children had become her life. She was more wary of Albert.

Flora looked embarrassed as she fell into the chair. He began his cries of 'More', whilst still applauding, even though the others had stopped. She simply had to sing it again. He had to hear it again. Her mother joined in the encouragement and she stood again, resigned to his wishes. This time, it was even more beautiful, he was carried away by the words. She was truly enchanting. She had worn a pale turquoise dress for her performance and it seemed to him that her dark eyes really shone at night. She wore a row of fine pearls around her white neck and a shawl of blue satin material that seemed to catch the air around her as she sang. She stood before him with the voice of a song thrush in an air-blue gown. His applause at the end was rapturous. She would not sing again despite his pleadings.

Before this, there had been some comedy of errors. She had worked all day at the farm, there was much to do that day as one of the best milkers was sick. Hackett had tied it in the yard after milking and the lady vet had been to tend it. It was one of the older cows on its fourth or fifth calf and it had diarrhoea. The yard smelt bad all day. Her final job before leaving to pick up the boy had been to collect the eggs and the hens had been roaming, so it took longer than she thought. It had been a hard day and her uniform was muddy but she meant to change as soon as she had driven him home. She was late and broke into a trot across the yard. Her fall into the mess the sick cow had left was inevitable. She slipped and it splattered everywhere. She rose to her knees with it all over her, even in her hair and she did not know whether to laugh or cry. Amy made up her mind for her, coming out of the farmhouse and seeing her there, covered in the stuff. She instantly began laughing and pointing. The commotion brought Hackett out and all three were creased with laughter at Flora's wretched state.

There was nothing she could do about it. She was late as it was. She wiped off what she could in the pump in the farmyard and hurried off to drive to the aerodrome.

'Whatever will he think of me,' she thought as she drove into the field. She had got used to the smell by now, but it was still overpowering. She drove up to his hangar. From where a black man suddenly ran out, hurled an oily rag he was carrying back at some unseen assailant and walked up to the car. She got out and looked at him, standing before her, covered in engine oil, his dark laughing eyes peering out from his black shiny face, and then down at her own manure covered breeches and the two of them just laughed together until their ribs ached.

'Whatever will my Mother say?' He looked her up and down; there were smudges of thin brown manure on her boots, her knees, her elbows and a streak of it across her hat. He had been practically drowned in oil by Maxwell and Knaggs. It had begun innocently enough with an oil rag being thrown around the hangar, but these things had a habit of escalating. In fact, Albert took an intense pride in escalating them himself. Maxwell and Knaggs were as black and oily as he was, hiding from him in some corner of the hangar.

She waited for him outside the ablutions hut whilst he made himself respectable enough to meet his family. She cleaned her hat but had all but given up on the state of her breeches. When he came out, he was shiny and clean, his hair combed, his uniform smart. For him, it had been a real effort. She admired her fresh faced fighting boy.

On the way to St Albans in the car they had talked so much. She had been told by Piper that he was quiet and shy, yet today she struggled to get a word in edgeways. He wanted her to know all about his family and where he lived. It felt like he was giving her a crash course in his life for an exam. He loved his people dearly. He positively glowed when he talked about his mother and his father. He made it quite clear he saw his efforts at the Front as something he was doing for them.

She bathed when she got home and changed into evening clothes whilst he spent time with Bill, her younger brother. Bill was an impressionable young man with a desire to go to the war, although he was just 16 and mercifully that was not about to happen. Mother had made a special tea. She was a wonder when it came to finding hard to get food items, the butcher had to continually remind her that there was a war on. Today she had managed to find halibut from somewhere. Albert had not seen fresh fish like that for a long time. The trawlers had been used in the war effort; there were few of them fishing now. It was agreed by all to be a very fine supper.

Then they had moved into the drawing room. Albert had begun the proceedings by playing his violin. What he lacked in skill, he made up for in enthusiasm. She had enjoyed his Schubert, even though mother had to race to keep up with him on the piano.

And then she had sung. And he had remembered that he loved her and that he had been thinking about her all day. She asked him if he'd like to see their garden and he said he would. Their house looked right out onto the town hall and the market place, so the garden was small. Bill had chaperoned them but had gallantly turned his back on them to look at the roses. They had a moment's opportunity for intimacy and he clasped her hand again. He had looked into her eyes then and she had fluttered a little, somewhere deep inside.

'You sing beautifully' he had said.

'Why thank you,' she replied. 'And you play well.'

He had such an urge to kiss her, to kiss those full red lips and run his fingers through her dark and flowing hair, but he would not, could not, and must not.

Instead he put all his emotions into one simple word.

'Bobs.' He touched her cheek with his finger and her eyes seemed to reflect fire.

Then Mrs Young called them from the house to tell them the tea was ready. They moved apart, she left his air and went back inside. He allowed himself a long glance at the moon which stood white and still above the garden, until a cloud blew across it. He and Bill joined them, in the warmth of the parlour.

9.

Monday May 7th 1917 Vert Galant Aerodrome.

She stood there, impervious to the three surgeons who surrounded her; his rigid brown kestrel that could tear through the air and spout gushes of blood. Ten years ago she could not have existed; twenty years ago she was just an idea; the newest, sharpest, fastest bird in the air. Her great wings hung over them, draping them in her shadow whilst they worked. She was every inch his hawk. She had arrived in crates and he had built her, then modified and re-modified and changed and straightened and hammered and replaced. He had unscrewed and screwed every bolt and nut inside of her. He knew every seam, every taut wire and wooden strut.

She had been individually kitted out by him, for him. She fitted the contours of his body intimately. She was his machine. His hands were inside her even now. He was totally absorbed in her. Paying deep attention to her movements, he deftly altered the way she would fly for him; a change that only he could possibly notice. His hands moved in a precise and measured way as he took parts from her, inspected them, cleaned and restored them. Now he had made her whole again, he mounted her proudly.

'Petrol on'. Charlie and Ted moved to the front of the plane.

'Petrol on' Charlie waited until he saw the petrol emerge from the cylinder then he called 'Petrol off'.

'Petrol off' called Ball and Charlie rotated the great wooden prop three times. Charlie was the swinger; he took get pride in his swing: if there had been a medal for the best swing in the squadron, he would have won it. In fact, if there had been an Olympic event that involved swinging a six foot long wooden propeller, he'd have won the gold medal every time. He aimed to swing 360° and did it nine times out of ten. This was a fine art; there were other swingers who'd lost hands, arms or the top half of their body by getting it wrong. You needed a good man to pull you clear, and in Ted, Charlie had the top man.

85

'Contact' sang Ball. Charlie's great powerful shoulders tensed then he swung. It was a beautiful swing, one of his best. He and Ted stepped back, their dance completed. The only thing missing was the roar of the engine. Despite the wonder of the swing and the attention and love she had been given, she stood idle, refusing to play.

'I told them at Candas not to restore the default settings on the engine. They always do. She's running too rich as it is. Let's get at the front of her and see what we can do.' Ball skipped down from the cockpit. His surgeons tools were laid out on a table beside her and he busily prepared her now. Candas was the Doctors where he had taken the bird two days ago, just a ten minute flight from the aerodrome. She had been shot to pieces and he had limped her over there to be made whole again.

Charlie stepped forward. 'You sure about that Sir, you're up in her in two hours time and you'll want to check her over completely before that.' As soon as he said it, he knew he should have bitten his tongue rather than speak. He had found out very quickly that there was absolutely no point whatsoever in trying to argue about aeroplanes, engines or anything else with Ball.

Ball did not even look up at him. 'You start on the radiator Ted and Charlie take the prop off and check the nosecone.'

'Right away, Sir.' The three of them busily and silently tended to her again. Charlie began working on the nosecone, following the sequence logically that was bullet pointed in his mind. He had started working on car engines as soon as he left school and then moved on to flying ones when war came. Both his brothers had ended up in the P.B.I, the Poor Bloody Infantry; he was so grateful that he had secured a place in the RFC. Now he was a mechanic in the best squadron, the new 56th. Blomfield had taken him out to dinner whilst the squadron was being formed. He had said he was looking for the best mechanics around, who could work on a new regiment of scouts; a super combat regiment that were to operate offensively in the forthcoming battle of Arras. Major Blomfield was a very persuasive man. Charlie seemed to think it had taken one beer, two bottles of red wine and several brandies for him to be persuaded.

Then there were the thirty new mechanics. The story went that Blomfield had got all the best mechanics and riggers in the RFC, including a lot of men who could play in the band. In fact, he recruited the band before the best mechanics. Then with the squadron expecting to be mobilised to France any minute, Blomfield was told by Wing he'd got too many experienced mechanics, he had to replace thirty of them with less experienced men. Lieutenant 'Bert' Charles was the top mechanic in the squadron; he'd got an honours degree in engineering before he was twenty, and was probably the best mechanical mind in the army at that time.

One day, two Lorries full of mechanics arrive at Shenley; it's the thirty replacements for the thirty good ones Blomfield is stalling on sending away. And what a rum lot they are, completely green, all of them. It would take months to train them up to work on the SE5s.

Blomfield and Bert put their heads together, then get the mechanics out of the lorry and take them to the tent where they'll be billeted. They don't go in themselves but tell the lads to make themselves at home. The mechanics go in and unpack and none of them realise it's the flu tent. There were four cases in there isolated with a nurse. Needless to say, they all got the flu and a fortnight off and Blomfield got to take all his good men with him to France.

It was Bert and Ball together, working deep into the night at London Colney aerodrome. They'd finally cooked the SE5 to make it the top-notch little fighter that

87

it was. Being in Ball's team was a blessing and a curse. He was a good chap, but took his work so seriously. He bought you gifts then hardly spoke all day. Some of the younger pilots knew nothing about engines at all. They went up in machines not really knowing how the thing got into the air. Ball knew every nut and bolt. He was an exact perfectionist, who could be very moody and change his mind when you least expected it. You worked long hours when you worked for Ball. There was one night there had been a space of exactly one hour, between the post flight checks of the night before and the pre-flight checks for his 3.30am patrol. To Ted and Charlie, it was their job, pure and simple whatever the time. Ball made sure that the two of them were bloody good at it. They took great pride in caring and restoring this modern wonder that was Ball's steed.

Now the three of them were bent over her again. The hangar did not exist for them, they saw only the engine. Someone clever had made her with a logic they needed to tap into. This would not beat them; they had too much pride for that. They seemed to spend their whole lives here, doing this. There was something unspoken yet agreed between them, there was nothing more important than this. Their lives were about making the great bird fly, nothing else.

Charlie was the first to notice the short figure of Blomfield enter the hangar. With any other pilot, the mechanic at this point was meant to say 'Hey up Sir, the C.O.s on his way,' and the pilot would then smarten himself up accordingly. But this was Ball. The rules no longer applied. Charlie glanced at Ball now who had seen the Major. Ball was wearing slippers and a mechanics overall, his mop of black hair as always, flecked with oil. Heaven only knows what his uniform looked like underneath. It usually looked like he'd slept in it, which he probably had, just in case a mad Hun came over in the middle of the night. You had to remember Ball lived in a hut like some odd cave dweller. He even lived in it after it had been on set on fire.

All three men saluted Blomfield and it was returned. He spoke like a man in a hurry. 'I'm just off to Savy Ball; we're talking about joint operations later today. You and Maxwell are up at 12.30, will you be ready?'

He had an air of curt efficiency and he was a good officer, one you could rely on. He was grey with a smart trimmed moustache. His uniform was immaculate, always. His cap would be just at the right angle, his belt and boots were polished. The three silver ribbons round the cuffs on his tunic were bright. His shirt and tie would be spotless and he had the bearing of a man who was always in control.

'We're going to work on the engine, she's not starting first swing and I think the mixture's too rich so we are going to sort that out, but we'll be ready Sir.' Ball smiled.

'That's the spirit, don't let me delay you'. Blomfield was already backing away. 'Tell your flight to be prepared for a sortie sometime later today. I'll meet with all three flight commanders at fifteen hundred hours, Cheer O Ball.' He turned and marched sharply away, his heels clicking.

'Cheer O Sir.' Ball returned to his table of marvellous instruments. Charlie and Ted returned to checking and adjusting; caressing and fondling the great brown bird. . The three figures bent over the machine in intense concentration. Outside the hangar, the first cloud of the morning began to creep across the sky.

Monday May 17th 1917 Hacketts Farm.

Flora straightened herself and looked up at the sky. It was beginning to cloud over. You relied on good weather all the time on the farm, but rarely got it. She looked at the ditch they had been digging. Her shoulders ached and she was developing a blister on her hand, but she was determined to get it done whilst it was fine. It would be no fun digging in the rain.

The four girls were spread out quite widely now across the bottom of the field. Hackett was digging alone at the top. He hadn't spoken to the girls since they found the box. Flora was relieved by this. She thought of the other Flora and this inspired her to dig deeper, ignoring the smart of the blister.

At school, they'd once been asked to write an essay for a prize called 'The woman I most admire.' Every one she knew wrote about Florence Nightingale or Elizabeth Fry. Flora had written about Mary Read, who'd gone to sea dressed like a man and became a successful pirate. Her essay hadn't won and if she could write it again now, she would change it. She'd write about the other Flora, Flora Sandes.

She'd first read about her in the papers. It was such a strange story. An English woman fighting alongside the men in the Serbian army; she hadn't understood how that could be. Then her Mother had wanted to go to the Albert Hall to see a concert. Clara Bow was on the bill and Flora admired her voice greatly. The Albert Hall had such wonderful acoustics, the concert had been splendid. This was back in February before she'd met or heard of Ball.

After the interval there had been a collection for the 'Sandes-Haverfield Canteen Fund' and Flora Sandes came on stage. She was a tall woman with curly hair under a Serbian army cap. She wore a khaki tunic with two medals pinned on it, khaki breeches and black boots. She was every inch a soldier. Sandes described her story to an interviewer, and Flora listened, deeply impressed by this woman.

Sandes had joined up as a nurse in 1914 and was so horrified by the primitive conditions she found in Serbia. After three months, she returned to England to raise money for a people she had fallen for. The Daily Mail had taken up her campaign so that the next time she returned to Serbia she took two thousand pounds worth of medical supplies with her. She had developed a passion for the Serbs, and when fighting got particularly bad, there were no ambulances so she could not help, she took off her Red Cross armband and offered it to Colonel Militch, He was the commanding Officer of the Serbian 'Iron regiment' and she wanted to become a regular private. Peasant girls had served in the army before and she was accepted there. They called her 'Our Englishwoman'. She joined his regiment as a new fighter, a woman going to war.

She fought her way across Macedonia and into Albania. The Serbian army was losing its war. She dug trenches alongside the men. She defended those trenches with her carbine; it was lighter than a rifle. She withdrew with the men and retreated with the men. She attacked with the men, running alongside them across No mans land and into machine gun fire. She defended the men in her regiment and fought a rearguard action to allow them to escape. She ate with them, slept next to them, and gave her all for them.

And how they loved her for it, 'Our Englishwoman' was willing to give her life for someone else's country. She was a shining light to them all. She was promoted to Corporal and was presented with the Sveti Sava medal, which she now wore, by the Prince regent of Serbia. Then the Serbs had run out of continent to hide and fight in.

91

When the Serbian army was withdrawn to Corfu, conditions had been really bad. They lacked even basic supplies, at one time 150 men were dying every day. Their bodies were transported across a black sea to the isle of death. These once brave fighters were starving now, becoming a bedraggled group of starving refugees that no one knew what to do with, except Flora. She fought for them there too. She argued and wrote letters to every authority she could think of. She pleaded, shouted and prayed. She forced the authorities to release all the supplies the army needed. They were nursed back to health and then became an army again.

Fighting alongside her men in Macedonia, she had been hit by an enemy grenade. She was temporarily blinded. It took three men to drag her back across No mans land to safety. Each of them was willing to risk their own lives for hers. She described lying there on the stretcher, her clothes had been ripped to pieces by an over-enthusiastic Medical Orderly and the stretcher was wet with blood. The journey to the Dressing station took two hours through the snow. They gave her half a bottle of brandy and a cigarette before she set out, to make sure she'd make it.

She didn't feel the cold, until the end of the journey and by then it numbed her sufficiently, to let the surgeon cut bits of the bomb out of her without any anaesthetic. She buried her head in the Doctor's broad chest and screamed with the pain. He looked at her and said:

'Remember, you are a soldier.' Then he placed a cigarette in her mouth and let her get on with it.

The journey down the mountain on a stretcher, and sometimes on a mule, took two days. Gradually, her sight had returned and she did her best not to curse too much. She was taken to Hospital in Salonica. There she was given a second medal, the Kara

George medal, the highest order in the Serbian army which carried with it automatic promotion to sergeant-major. Her doctors had ordered her back to England for a rest and further operations. She had used the time to raise more funds.

The crowd in the Hall rose to their feet and cheered on hearing her story. Men dug deep to find donations for her that night. Afterwards, she had sat at the side of the stage and enjoyed the concert. Sergeant major Flora Sandes nodded her head to the music and tapped her feet. Flora Young watched her all evening. She was determined to speak to her by the night's end. She made her way down to her during the encore. She told her mother to wait for her at the end.

When the final applause ended, Flora Sandes stood accepting a cheque from a grey haired gentleman. She smiled as Flora approached and they shook hands. She had rehearsed what to say in her head, as she waited, and hoped it came out now as she spoke:

'Miss Sandes erm Sergeant Sandes, I just wanted to thank you for what you have done for women.'

Sandes looked perplexed then broke into a smile.

'Women? I haven't done anything for the women dear, I fight with the men, marvellous Serbian men.' She was ushered away by the rest of her party as Flora struggled in her mind, to explain what she had meant.

To her way of thinking, before the war, women had been fighting to be recognised as equals by throwing themselves under horses, chaining themselves to railings or starving themselves to death. She'd grown up hearing these stories about women her mother admired for making a stand, and her father thought peculiar. Now women were showing what they could do. The other Flora had done her bit, just as hundreds of thousands everywhere were doing theirs, right now.

As she returned through the emptying stalls to her mother she wrestled further with the idea. She could not have fought in battles, even if the Government suddenly started calling up women to the trenches, which would never ever happen. But one woman had and in doing so had shown how it could be done.

And so now she dug and whilst digging, she prayed for an end to the war, the return of the sunshine and the peace and her man.

10.

Saturday October 21st 1911 Trent College, Long Eaton, Derbyshire

Mr John Saville Tucker stood, and all the boys rose with him from their benches. His withering eye looked down the rows of them standing either side of the long wooden tables and forced each head to bow. The Hall was panelled in deep dark oak; Tucker was raised up on the Master's platform and was resplendent in his red gown. He would not begin until all coughing and scraping had subsided. He had told them on many separate occasions that he was quite prepared to stand there all day if necessary, he would not say Grace over any noise at all. His predecessors, some of them not as kindly disposed towards the boys as he was, looked down on them all from portraits on the walls. Trent had a history of moulding gentlemen and Tucker felt the boys needed to be aware and proud of that. He began:

'Father in heaven we thank thee for all thy kindnesses to us and ask thee to help us labour this day to be more worthy of thy great favour to us. For what we are about to receive, may we be extremely grateful. Amen.' All the masters and boys said Amen together then sat to eat their porridge.

Albert liked Saturdays at Trent best of all. Most of the boys got involved in sports in the grounds. There was a football match today between the first eleven and a team from Bluecoats school, so the carpentry shop would be quiet. Last week, he, Cyril and Todd had been the only ones in there all day. He was working on an electric motor launch. He had drawn the plans himself, the first set of plans he had managed to draw accurately. He thought it should be able to carry a cargo of up to 48 pounds. Today they were going to cut out the rails for the sides.

Before that, they had to endure the long walk that Tucker had decreed should take place that morning. The whole college would turn out and follow Tucker in a brisk march round the school field and then through the town and down to the river. The masters led by example, except the ones at the back who were there to look out for any dawdlers. Tucker could not abide dawdlers. Last time there had been a walk; three boys got a swishing from his cane for that offence. Albert and Cyril employed

95

their usual tactics of staying firmly in the middle of the hundred marching boys, catching occasional snippets of conversation about planes, lathes and engines. By lunchtime they were back in the hall for lunch which today was a watery soup and hunk of bread. Tucker explained to the parents on Open Evening that their £75 a year fee meant the boys were given adequate nourishment but not indulged. The school tuck shop was a thriving business as a result.

Now the time was their own, and Albert and Cyril made their way to the carpenter's shop. The afternoon was fair and they could hear the rest of the school cheering the match, down on the field. The shop was lined with wooden cabinets with glass doors where the tools were kept. On top of the cabinets were boxes, a guitar, a rocking horse, all in various stages of production. There were solid wooden benches, the surface of them full of cuts and nicks where boys had inexpertly tied to plane, chisel, saw or hammer. The benches were equipped with a vice each side and had a recess cut into them where other tools were stored. The room had a rich smell of sawdust which often covered the floor, but today they found it clean and knew to leave it that way as well. The woodwork teacher allowed the usage of the room as long as his rules were adhered to.

Albert reached up and took his launch from the top of a cabinet. They placed it on the bench behind them and bent down to study it closely.

'We'll build the side rails first Cill and stick them on, then work on the roof of the engine house.' He looked proudly over the wooden launch they had been working on for weeks now. It was well made and the timbers were a good deep colour. The boat was more than two feet long and the underside curved roundly as a testament to the hours they had spent with the plane.

Albert selected two strips of dark wood from the bin placed behind the lathe. He used a metal rule and a wooden square to draw out the shape he needed with a pencil then tried to smoothly draw in the curves it required. Cyril mimicked his every movement. Their efforts were concentrated and thoughtful.

Todd entered the room:

'Afternoon Ball and Ball, how's the boat coming along.' He was one of the twenty boys that shared F dormitory them and at first had joined in all the projects they were working on, like the Ark last spring, but he soon became bored and abandoned them. Albert and Cyril showed him the boat which he admired and complimented. Then he put on his apron and took the chair leg he was making for his mother to the lathe.

The cheering outside grew louder, it sounded like the team was winning again. Both of the Ball boys had tried their hand at all the many sports the college offered but with little success. Albert won an Obstacle race on Sports day through determination, rather than skill. He simply kept going while the faster runners fell over. It was the only thing either boy won at Trent. He carefully sawed the wood down to the pencil line, and then began to chisel out the pattern. He looked over at Cyril's efforts and was pleased to see that the shape matched his own.

They were interrupted by a whining noise coming from Todd's lathe. Then they could hear the strap banging wildly against the machine. Todd, ham-fisted as ever had managed to break the strap. The master would be furious; he was given little for repairs. Todd looked down on the machine in bewilderment. He'd really done it this time. He made a snap decision, unscrewed the wood he was working on and extricated himself and his work from the scene. He pulled the apron off over his head in one movement, called 'Goodbye Balls, I'll explain it to Mr Williams on Monday,' and then hurried back to his dorm.

Albert and Cyril made their way over and looked at the stricken machine. The strap had snapped completely and would have to be replaced. Albert decided to remove it and place it on the master's desk where he would be sure to discover it. He was holding the thing in his hand when the older boys bundled into the room.

Albert had seen them around the school many times before but never spoken to them. They were in their final year so were all aged between 17 and 18. The ring leader was a tall blond boy. He had a henchman who never left his side, a fat freckled boy with ginger hair; a mean looking angry boy. The two of them followed by four others rounded on him now as he stood there holding the strap.

'Well, well, what have we here, Williams won't like this at all, will he boys? You've smashed the strap on his best lathe.'

'It wasn't me, 'Albert heard himself saying pathetically. 'I was just...'

The ginger boy grabbed him by the ear and tugged it hard. Albert winced at the pain.

'Wasn't me' the ginger boy imitated him in a girl's voice. 'Who was it then, your little girl friend over there?' Two of the boys grabbed Cyril, one on each arm and they dragged him over to Albert. The blond one turned on him again.

'Right boys, I think we've found two miserable little squealers who need teaching a lesson. I think a damn good thrashing is in order.' The others laughed at the suggestion. Albert called out:

'Leave him alone, we didn't do it. We were just...' He was interrupted by a sharp slap on the side of the head from the ginger boy. Albert was dragged from the lathe to a bench and forced to bend over it. The ginger boy's fat hand pressed his head down into the wood. Their were tears in his eyes as he came up with his final efforts to stop what was about to happen;

'Leave him alone, it was me, I did it.' The response showed his calculations had not worked.

'Right then boys, let's thrash them both.' The blond boy went to the wood bin and removed two rods of dowel. He tried them out in the air first and they swished menacingly. He handed one to a darker boy, grinning behind him who went over to where Cyril was being pushed by his face into the bench. Cyril was crying openly, but Albert would not give them the satisfaction.

'I think a good ten strokes on the bare backside with a decent run-up should just about do it, hey Creggs.' Both boys removed their jackets and began to role up their sleeves. The anger in Albert was fierce but he could find no words to say now, his face betrayed his righteous anger that they were to suffer this. One of the boys pulled down his trousers, he tried to kick out but they were too big and he was being held either side. One of the boys whistled at him, 'I say, that's a pretty one'. The other boys laughed.

'Right, a four step run-up should do it, I'll go first.' He heard the blond boy walk back behind him. One of the ones holding him giggled. Then there was the sound of black boots running across wood for four quick steps, each creaking closer, a loud swish of rod through air and the pain convulsed through him. He let out a gasp full of uncontrollable anger. They laughed.

'Nice one Scottie, you've made a super stripe. That one will still be there next week. Go on Creggs.' He heard the boots running again. He could hear Cyril's anguished breathing. When the rod hit him he cried aloud. Then the sobs shook through him.

Albert gritted his teeth. His chest was knotted with it; he tried not to tense his muscles, fearing it would hurt even more. They counted each stroke now. It was becoming a great game. The second one was worse than the first, it smarted and stung. His backside felt on fire. Cyril screamed at the second one then grunted at each subsequent stroke. In between his sobbing became quieter.

He tried to sun up all his strength and shouted:

'You are being bloody beastly; we did not break the lathe, another boy, Todd…' His cries were in vain, the boy holding his right arm smashed his forehead on against the bench to silence him, the laughter continued.

By the ninth stroke, the pain was acute but he found himself rising above it on a wave of righteous anger. He could bear this beating, he knew, but Cyril was much smaller than he was and had stopped crying out with each stroke. For the boys with the rods it had become a competition to make the best stroke marks on each boy. They had given the other boys, who up until now had just been their captors, their own go. The final one was to be the best of all from his blond tormentor. He missed the backside completely and cut a swathe across the tops of Albert's thighs. He drew blood which Albert could feel running down his leg. The other boys cheered. Then for reasons Albert never understood, he took the rod and whirled it like a conductor's baton. Albert felt the point of the cane penetrate him. He felt sick and cried like a baby.

Then, in a flurry of laughter, they were gone and he and Cyril were alone in the workshop crying. He pulled himself up and pulled his trousers up, wiping off the spot of blood with his finger. He went over to Cyril and hugged him. He held the crying boy and helped him pull his trousers up. Then the two of them wiped their eyes, put the boat away and walked back to the dorm without speaking.

Cyril was still sobbing a little. Albert took him to his bed, helped him undress and then tucked him in. A plan was forming in his mind. His own bed was next to Cyril's and he began emptying the contents of his cupboard into his little brown leather suitcase. He would show them, he would not be treated like that. Cyril was asleep when it was time for tea at five. With the masters and boys safely in the Hall, now was Albert's time. He took the book on engineering he had borrowed from the school library and stepped outside, clutching his suitcase. He wrapped the scarf Lol had knitted him round his chin for warmth and comfort. His progress down the long gravel drive and into the town went unnoticed.

He talked to himself just a little when there was no one about as he made his way to the station. He could stay no longer in this place that had defiled him. Once he had gone, his parents would come and rescue Cyril. He had been saving up his allowance to buy engine parts for the boat; he had enough money to get to London maybe. He caught the train from Long Eaton to Nottingham Midland Station and on the platform there, he made his decision. The next train out went to Liverpool. He bought a ticket, crossed the platforms and got on it.

The journey to Liverpool was a long one; the train seemed to stop in a hundred places he had never heard of before. The compartment now was busy, but he kept to himself and read his book, wrapping his scarf round him. He became used to the rhythm of the train's journey. The guard's whistles at each station, the ladies in hats who alighted and the conductor's winks as he checked the tickets.

Finally the train arrived in Liverpool Lime Street and he walked down the dark platform, past the steaming engine. From the gates of the station, he could see the Mersey River and he walked towards it. It was after ten at night and a lone boy might attract a curious policeman so he walked briskly along the river, past the Liver building and towards the Albert Docks. The docks were quiet, the boats unguarded and he had his pick of them as he walked along.

The next part was the one he knew would be the hardest. He had read some months ago, that America always needed engineers and he felt sure that someone there would recognise that he was special; that he had the power to coax life out of an engine that others had given up on. He knew he would miss his mother, but intended to write to her once he was there. She would understand why he couldn't go back to Trent, why he couldn't face again those boys who had done that to him. His backside had stung all the way and still felt warm, hours later.

He watched the empty gangplanks of the boats tied up in the dock for half an hour. He was hungry and tired. He chose a big paddle steamer, which he hoped was bound for New York the next day. The crew were asleep and he crawled quietly up the gangplank. He crept across the deck and took a set of wooden steps down into the belly of the boat. He walked on tiptoe along a wooden corridor, and then entered the room at the end. It was the engine room, a perfect place for him.

He studied the great steam engine. It was a huge steel box with pipes rising out of it. Along the side were levers and handles and dials. The engine was sleeping now and all the noise you could hear was the faint lap of the water against the side of the boat. He had found the perfect place. The engine room was warm and dark and he felt safe there. He found sacks of coal he could use for bedding and pulled up his suitcase next to him. He thought briefly of poor Cyril and his mother before he fell asleep, his head wrapped in the scarf Lol had made.

The chief engineer found the stowaway next morning. He asked the boy what he was doing there but the boy was inarticulate and could not explain. The police were called, who called his father. Albert Senior had risen to Mayor of Nottingham for the year. He cancelled all his mayoral duties for the day and came up to get him in the train. He found the boy sitting in the police station, still covered in coal dust. He made him wash, before they went back to the station. He explained to the boy how foolish, he'd been, he'd worried his mother so. The family had not been expecting this at all. It had been a shock to them all, especially his mother. The boy was wracked with guilt at this. He was returned to Trent, on the understanding that this would never happen again.

Many times after that, he saw the boy who had beaten him around the college but he became well practised at forgetting. He put the events of that day out of his mind for good.

Wednesday April 27th 1917. Hacketts Farm.

They had finished the evening milking and the dairyman, or rather dairymaid had been and fetched the full silver churns and taken them away on her cart, there was quiet on the farm. Hackett was in the dairy, making cheese with Beatrice and Violet; he had asked the other girls to clean out the shed where he kept his bull. Flora had been so wary of it at first. It had great grey horns and a disconcerting habit of staring you straight in the eye. It was a real beast, forever finding ways to get out of its stall and go off in search of the cows. Used to it now, she had tethered in securely in the yard whilst the two girls began bringing out spades full of acrid smelling straw and manure, which they had now formed into a great steaming mound.

The birds were beginning their evening chorus and the pigeons were flying in and out of the yard. They had made their nests in the more dilapidated buildings. The bull gave a guttural snort from time to time, but then came another sound, one which seemed alien in the environs of the farm. It was an engine

In the sky, there was something flying towards them. There had been several Zeppelin raids recently and although Amy knew it was unlikely that they would stray this far from London, all the Land Army girls were on strict orders to report anything unusual in the air. Now with dusk falling around her, Amy shaded her eyes with one hand and looked into the sky.

Once she had seen it, a grey speck flying from the South of them towards the farm she pointed it out to Flora.

'Is it one of ours?' she asked. Flora looked carefully up at the plane which was getting nearer all the time. She could see from the shape that it was a bi-plane, a small single seater. She could see no markings but there was excitement rising within her. Planes meant something special to her now.

'I think so, it looks like a scout'. Amy shot a sideways glance at Flora, you could never tell what she might know or not know but this knowledge of aircraft was something new. The plane was more or less directly above them now and Amy was certain that it had begun circling the farm. The sound of it seemed so out of place. The engine wailed above them as the plane got lower in the sky. Flora was transfixed, following the machine with her eyes. As it flew lower, she could see the pilot wore

no helmet, there was the familiar mop of black hair.

'I think it's my friend' she said and Amy was once more amazed. Flora had lots of

friends Amy knew, but she had never mentioned a flyer. The plane was getting lower

and lower with every circle. The pilot waved at the girls and Flora waved back. Her

heart was pounding away by now. The plane flew over the yard in a final circle just a

few feet above the buildings and then went out of sight, over the trees into the lower

field. They heard the engine come to a halt and then both girls ran to where it must

have landed.

Amy arrived first. The pilot was turning off the engine. He jumped down from the

cockpit. This was the nearest Amy had ever been to a flying machine. It was smaller

than she had imagined. The pilot was a young lad; he had a red face and jet black

hair. He smiled at her.

'Cheer O, is this Hackett's farm?' And then as Flora approached he added 'Ahh, I can

see it is, Cheer O Bobs!'

Flora was breathless and as flushed as he was. She looked down at the uniform she

had worked in all day and its various layers of mud and grime. 'Albert, how lovely to

see you, but you should have telephoned first!'

He smiled and walked over to her. He grasped Flora's hand and Amy noted the

familiarity between them. 'I wasn't sure I'd get here at all. The winds getting up a bit

and the only landmark I had to look for were a herd of Friesian cows.'

'This is Amy Carmichael Albert; she shares a room with me here. Amy, this is

Captain Ball.' He shook Amy's hand but said nothing. Amy smiled back at him; she glanced at the medal ribbons on his crumpled tunic. This must be the one she had read about in the papers, they were being visited by a celebrity.

The noise of the plane landing had brought Hackett out of the dairy with Beatrice and Violet following. Hackett spent some time looking over the plane after an introduction that neither man felt particularly comfortable with. Whilst he admired the marvels of flight, he somehow resented the war bird being parked in his field. He had done all he could to keep the war away from his farm. He invited the young pilot to take tea with them in the farmhouse kitchen. They trooped back across the yard.

Albert sat in the guest of honours place at the top of the big table. The girls arranged themselves in rows so they might look at the famous 'marvel of the air' who'd come to visit them. Only Violet remained truculent and unimpressed.

Beatrice asked him what it was like flying in combat, but he said little. His face coloured continually and he squirmed a little in his chair. Hackett wanted to know what the Front looked like from the air. Ball mumbled a description of two lines of trenches, about thirty yards apart. Things improved considerably when Beatrice offered him some of the fruit cake she had made; he at last became more animated. They drank their tea from the white china cups and Ball fiddled with the teapot. Flora took control of the conversation now, telling the others how they'd met and how he had taken her on a flight. With the exception of Violet, the others were suitably impressed.

Once the ordeal of the tea was over, Flora suggested she showed Albert the farm and he seemed eager. Hackett had vague thoughts that he should chaperone them but dismissed them, it might be more comfortable for everyone, if they were just left alone together. It was a relief when the two of them clattered the latch on the farmhouse door and walked across the yard.

'Well,' said Violet, 'she keeps things quiet. Captain Ball, the marvel of the air and our Flora, who'd have thought it.' The other girls watched them walk across the farmyard with a sort of hidden awe.

The first place she took him was to the bull's stall with its huge mound of manure they had collected outside. She joked with him. This is all my and Amy's work she said pointing to it and laughing.

'Really?' he asked. 'I told you that you should eat more greens!' They laughed together; he was impressed by the bulls' horns and its great big pink shiny nose. 'I wanted to come yesterday, next Saturday seems a very long time to wait to see you again, but I had to fly a new plane back from Farnborough and there just wasn't time.' He looked quite dashing today she thought, and she was so grateful he had come. 'It is all right isn't it Bobs? He nodded towards the farmhouse; 'They seem like a good lot. I never like meeting new people, never know what to say.'

She admired him then; he was like a little lost boy sometimes. A bunch of broody hens scattered as they past them, pecking at the foot of a haystack.

'Well, I haven't had time to tell them about you, so now they will be asking questions.' She noticed the dusk drawing in around them. 'Will you be all right flying back? Won't it be dark?'

He smiled at her. 'It's not far, just the other side of St Albans. I can follow the roads back; the blackout has taken away all the useful lights to navigate by.' Then there came a silence between them. She wanted to say how good it was to see him, but struggled to find the words. As they walked back down to the field he took her arm in hers and it felt good. The words formed simply for her.

'It is so good to see you. I so hoped we might spend more time together, thank you for flying to see me.' He grinned.

'I wanted to ask you something. I wondered if you'd come to the airfield for tea tomorrow. I wanted to know... I wondered if you would write to me, when I go to France I mean. Letters mean so much to a chap out there.'

She stopped walking and smiled at him. He was such an enigma to her. This boy who could fly like a bird, who wielded the power of life and death over engines, who had shot down more enemies than any other Englishman, and yet who struggled to make simple conversation, over tea in a farmhouse.

'I'd be delighted to come for tea tomorrow. And of course I'll write to you, you didn't need to ask. There is one thing though, one thing I must tell you. I can't bake a cake to save my life.' He laughed.

'Nobody's perfect, my mother and sister bake me far too many cakes as it is.' They looked over the gate into the cows' field. One great black and white beast, her flanks splattered with manure looked up at them and gave a warning moo before lazily munching on a clump of buttercups. Albert mooed back at her and the pair laughed again. A light breeze blew and Albert looked concerned.

'The winds getting up, I had better get back.' As they walked through the field back to the house, he spotted a white horn shaped flower in the hedgerow. He picked it for her and placed it under her hat, behind her ear. She was still wearing it when they entered the farmhouse. The other girls looked at it and she snatched it away and put it in a glass of water.

'Mr Hackett, I wondered if you'd be my swinger this evening,' said Albert, more at ease now. 'What's that?' asked Hackett. He joined them as they made their way back to the plane, and the other girls came too to see the thing take off.

Albert spent a few minutes explaining to Hackett how to swing the prop and not get caught by it. Then he showed Flora how to start the engine, using the switch under his cockpit. Then he held her hand once more and said,
'Cheer O chap; see you tomorrow and no bad smell this time.'

She giggled. 'I'll try and stay away from the manure until I see you again.' Then they went through the sequence as he'd showed them. Hackett was delighted with himself when his swing brought the machine into whirring life. Ball turned and winked at her, saluted them all, then bumped across the field and roared off into the night.

Back in the farmhouse she took the white flower and placed it next to her bed where she could see it, and dreamt of him all through the night.

11.

Sunday August 9th 1914. Sedgeley House, Nottingham

'But Harriet love, the army will be the making of the boy. Everything has changed now, its war Harriet. We can't go on pretending it's not happening. The Germans are right now marching through Belgium, burning and looting the towns. We have to set an example, the call has gone out for a hundred thousand men and our Albert will be one of them, the first to answer it'.

Ball Senior turned his back on his wife and gazed out of the window and down the garden. He took a cigar from his waistcoat pocket and lit it. The argument had not changed for three days, it had already been decided and Fred would be here any moment so they could go and prepare for the meeting together. He knew how much Harriet was devoted to the lad, but it was right and just that the boy should go to the war, Albert Senior knew it.

Mrs Alderman Ball, Nottingham's Lady Mayoress was unconvinced. She wrung the handkerchief that she was clutching. Her boys were the world to her and the war was threatening to take at least one of them away.

'He's not 18 for another three weeks Albert. He's not old enough to go overseas for another year. He's been doing so well at the works, can't it wait until he's old enough? Why does it have to be our son that we parade as an example?' She breathed a long sigh. The argument had been going on for days, ever since Albert Senior had had the idea and convinced the boy that he should be the first to go. The papers were all signed and sealed and sat on the table between them.

'It's just as Fred said, Harriet love, to make an example for the others. We can't expect other people's sons to go, if we are not willing to send our own. It's done now, and it will be a year before they can send him to Belgium, it will all be over by then.' He sat down beside her with an air of finality and wiped his brow. It was a hot day in what had been a hot summer. He flicked his cigar ash into the ashtray.

Although there had been talk of a European war for years, for Harriet it seemed to have all happened so suddenly. The assassination of a Duke she'd never heard of before, and then the slow burning fuse through July, the ultimatum to the Germans left unanswered and then war broke over her family like some great white wave. Now the wave threatened to sweep away the boys she loved so much. The clock ticked steadily away on the mantelpiece and the two sat in silence. There was little point in him endlessly repeating his enthusiasm and she her fears.

Two floors above them, but still able to catch the odd word of their argument, Albert had been looking through his bible. He was in the book of Exodus, reading Moses' song of triumph after the Israelites had crossed the Red Sea. He'd wanted to find the verses which showed that God approved of his decision. He'd found nothing in the book which said he shouldn't go and fight. He read Chapter 15 and stopped at verses two and three:

'The Lord is my strength and song; he has become my salvation: he is my God, and I will prepare him a habitation; my father's God, and I will exalt him. The Lord is a man of war: the Lord is his name.'

He underlined the verses with a pencil. For a moment he considered running downstairs and showing his mother. She might understand better if she could see that it was God's will he was doing. He knew she was worried about him signing up for the army but couldn't really see why. His father had first spoken to him about it, on Tuesday. By then it had already become inevitable. They had sat up waiting for the ultimatum to the Germans to be answered, which of course it never was. When the clock chimed 11, Father had looked at him:

'That's it Lad, it's done. We're at war. Will you go? I think you must.'

It had taken him no time at all to reply. He had spent so long in the Officer Training Corps at Trent, he knew what army life might be like. He had marched, drilled, pitched tents and dug trenches. He had fired his rifle from the armoury on the Robin Hoods' rifle range. It felt like he had completed the training already.

'Yes Father, I'll go.'

'That's the spirit Lad.' And that was that. Now he was anxious to do it. He wanted to see action as quick as he possibly could. He wanted to do the right thing and prove to his parents he was everything they wanted him to be. He had signed the papers to join the Robin Hoods. Then Uncle Fred had been to see him about the recruitment rally that evening. It would encourage the other men to join up if he would be willing to sit with his Mother on the stage and be introduced at the end of the speeches as the first man in Nottingham to answer Kitchener's call; the son of the Lady Mayoress and one of Nottingham's leading civic families. That part he dreaded. There might be more than a thousand people there at the rally and he knew his face would be beetroot red as soon as his name was mentioned, but his Uncle and his Father had convinced him, that this was all part of him doing his duty.

He heard heavy footsteps running up the stairs to his attic room. Lol burst in with a grin. She had been painting in her room, listening to the argument below and was full of it now.

'You've set them off again Albert! It's like our house has had its own war this week.' He smiled at her obvious enjoyment of the strife. She was an attractive young woman of twenty two with a stream of broken hearts behind her. She shared Albert's dark eyes. They had grown even closer since he had come back from College and begun work at the Universal Engineering Works in Castle Boulevard. Lol was working as a secretary in her father's estate agency in between her packed social calendar. They set out for work in the mornings together and regrouped round the dinner table at night.

'It's not my fault; I'm just doing what Father wants me to. Look here, how about you take my place on the stage tonight? You do look like a boy after all, I am simply dreading it.'

'You shy boy', she pinched his cheek. 'Oh no, I can't deprive the good people of Nottingham from seeing how good looking their latest war hero is. I think I'll suggest to Father that you go in uniform this evening, after all, I bet you'd still fit into your Scouts' one.'

'Don't you dare,' warned Albert as she bounded back out of his room.

The bell rang at four and Uncle Fred arrived, already dressed in his mayoral robes, the same ones his brother had worn four years before. He was ushered in by the maid and was carrying a rolled up poster. He spread it out on the table in front of them. It was a simple but direct message. It showed Kitchener, the hero of the Boer war pointing out of it and a simple slogan. 'Your country needs you.'

Albert Senior was impressed. 'That's a fine sentiment. Have they put them round the Hall?' Fred was taller than Albert but they were clearly brothers. He had the same waxed moustache, the same piercing eyes and the same way of standing with his back to the fire, his paunch protruding into the parlour.

'Oh yes, two hundred of them arrived yesterday from London. They are to be displayed at all the venues for the recruiting rallies. The Duke of Portland is due to arrive at six, so I thought we could take the carriage down to the Hall at five thirty. Is Harriet's speech ready?'

'I wrote it for her on Friday morning, but she has disputed it with me, Fred. She didn't like the word sacrifice and insisted I changed it. I can't see why as a sacrifice is exactly what we'll be asking the men to make and their families too. Other than that one word, she's ready.'

'And the boy?' Fred knew the boy's example would be an important part of that night's message.

'He's ready too, keen as mustard, although not keen on going on the stage; he asked if his mother might announce it with him in the audience. I told him, he has to be seen. He's setting a fine example and people will want to see him.' Albert Senior felt that this was the way things should be done; he liked everything to be just right.

They took the Mayor's carriage across the town. His mother wore her chains of Office and Uncle Fred waved proudly at passers-by. Albert was nervously chewing his fingernails until his father knocked them away from his mouth. When they pulled up outside the Albert Hall, there was already a great queue of people stretching right round the block. The Kitchener posters were everywhere. There was an atmosphere of enthusiasm and a feeling that this was the beginning of an adventure that would lead the fine men of Nottingham all the way to Berlin.

The boy's stomach was churning and churning. He tried to take a seat at the very back of the platform but his Uncle called him over to be presented to the Duke of Portland who was to speak first. They shook hands and the Duke congratulated him on being the first one to show willing to go. Albert felt that it was Father who deserved the congratulations; it had all been his idea. He was ushered to a seat on the second row of the stage, between his parents.

The Hall filled quickly; the first through the doors ran to fill the front row. There was every kind of family there, from the dignitaries in their gowns to the scruffy chaps in flat caps, still recovering from their lunchtimes in the pub. As the rows filled

Albert grew more and more nervous. Soon the Hall was full to overflowing. They were standing three deep at the back.

The entire Hall rose as one, once the orchestra had started the National anthem. To the boy, it seemed like the eyes of Kitchener were everywhere. There were soldiers with them on the platform and five recruiting Sergeants waited at their tables at various points round the Hall. The atmosphere gained momentum when they sang 'Rule Britannia'. The words had never seemed as relevant before as this.

Uncle Fred introduced the Duke and he spoke of England's need for men who were willing. He talked about the dark acts of depravity which even now, as he spoke, the Germans were inflicting on gallant little Belgium. What a great obligation Britain had to this little country defending itself against the might of Prussian oppression. He spoke of the example of Kitchener and the British army, who even now, as he spoke, were marching to Belgium's aid. He appealed to their fine senses of justice. He played on their consciences, he called on their sense of patriotism, and he forced them into a choice.

Some men were becoming anxious. Some queued at the tables before the speeches were even finished. Women in the hall were nervously giving their men sidelong glances. If they went, who would help bring up the child? Others were more encouraging, nodding sagely at each point of the speech, imagining in their minds the dark and terrible deeds of the Hun army and looking forward to the day when they could proudly say that their man had gone to the war.

After the Duke, the Mayor, and several leading citizens had added to the clamour for enlistment, it was Harriet's turn. She was being swept away by the excitement and read every word of the speech written for her including the sacrifice, over which she and her husband had argued. Albert Senior beamed with delight when she did that. Finally Uncle Fred came forward for the last time. He told the throng that he couldn't ask them to do something he was not willing for his own family to do, so the first man to sign up was introduced; he was the son of Lady Mayoress and Mr Alderman Ball, and his own nephew, Mr Albert Ball.

Albert rose slowly on cue, his cheeks burned hot, his hands were shaking and he sat down again before the crowd finished their applause. His Father reached over and patted him on the back proudly as the whole Hall rose to sing again. Albert felt Kitchener pointing directly at him, but the papers his Uncle had waved at the crowd were completed and he was already on board the great ship of enthusiasm that carried a Nation to war.

The final chorus of the National Anthem was a slightly more sombre one. The future hung unknown over all of them and despite all the Union Jacks and pointing Kitcheners; every man that signed up that night, every man whose eager hands shook as they were handed the pen, was someone's son, someone's father, someone's husband. There were some that left the Hall still civilians and went home to a night full of yearning. Whilst their children slept above them, they argued with the wife by gaslight, why they should or should not go.

It was a much relieved Albert that followed the mayoral party down from the platform and back out through the Hall. He had a certain quiet pride in his small contribution to the success of the evening. As he made his way through the crowd a tall woman approached. 'Well done Lad' she said and shook his hand vigorously. He felt his face flush once again. He watched a boy, trying to look older by wearing a bowler hat, but unmistakably still at school, slouch away from the recruiting table

116

rejected. His tears a clear sign that he was too young to go. Then came the best moment when he recognised Bob Thrale, standing patiently queuing, and Arthur Holmes with him. He went and shook hands with his old pals. It was a great feeling, to be in it together. They all talked at once, flushed with anticipation, they just couldn't wait to be in the thick of it. They were all up for the Robin Hoods so would fight the Hun together.

Back at home, his father took him to one side in the hallway, beside the deeply ticking clock:

'You've done well lad, you've done us proud. You know, there's a moment in every man's life when he has to make it for himself Albert, and this is your moment. Whatever happens in this war, and I hope it won't all be over before you can get there; you will always be able to say you did what was right, at just the right time to do it. Your mother's proud as punch and so am I. Well done lad.'

Albert's heart swelled. There was nothing he wanted to do more in the world than please his father. Now he wanted to get to the war just as quickly as he could. He dreamt that night of marching into Germany with Kitchener pointing the way to Berlin.

Friday January 19th 1917 Canning Town, London.

Amy gasped as the cold water ran through her hair. She could have waited for the water to heat up, but mother would be home soon and would want to go out. Mother's bottle of stout in their local on a Friday evening was something she looked forward to all through their long working week. Amy picked up the bar of Knights coal tar soap and began to run it through her long hair with her delicate long fingers.

117

Then she gasped again as she rinsed the lather away. She wrapped her dripping wet hair in a towel, which she twisted into a turban on top of her head. Then she went through into the bedroom she shared with her mother and began to vigorously dry it.

They had moved to the one bedroom basement flat from Greenwich two years ago. Mother's work as a seamstress had all but died out when the war started. People seemed to have less to spend, and many of her customers had been gentlemen who had long since gone to France. Amy liked to think that it was their patriotism that had led them to the munitions factory, a response to the shell shortage that the papers said was becoming critical, but in fact, it was necessity. They needed the work to survive.

Life for them had been a sad, slow decline. They had been relatively wealthy when her father was alive, he was a chemist and her mother had no need to work then, but there was an accident at his works and one day he never came home. Amy had been just thirteen at the time. Once they had paid for the funeral, there seemed little money left. Her mother had sewed and taken in laundry and for a while they managed to survive, but it had not lasted.

Amy examined her hair in the mirror above the bed they shared. She was certain it was changing. Her skin was gradually going yellow and her long blond curly locks had a definite orange tinge, she was sure of it. It happened to all the girls who worked with T.N.T. eventually. They breathed it in all day and it left its mark on them, it was such a deadly poison.

Eileen had been the first to go off sick. She was Amy's best friend at the factory and her skin had gone a deep yellow colour. Her hair went orange, like a clown. The works allowed Eileen a fortnight off sick, told her to rest, eat well and drink lots of milk. She came back looking much better. There were other symptoms that the girls had to suffer though, not just cosmetic ones.

There were girls in the Press Room that had no idea they were epileptic when they started but now fell to the floor, their mouths foaming in a deep fit, almost every day. Fainting was also quite common; her mother had fainted four times. Amy hadn't suffered from the faints, but she knew plenty of girls that had.

Although she had never worked anywhere else, Amy longed to escape the factory walls. She operated a milling machine making shell cases, and then sometimes she filled the cases with explosives. There were forty girls working in her section. The work was easy enough and the other girls were fun to be with, they gossiped the twelve hour shifts away; but Amy longed for fields and the open air. They worked days so she felt like sunlight was a pleasure denied her. She had always been so proud of her hair and the factory was ruining it. Now she brushed her damp hair, trying to remove the faint orange glow.

She was interrupted by loud knocking on the front door. It seemed urgent, almost frantic. It couldn't be mother; she had stayed to do an hour's overtime and had a key. She rushed to the door and there was Mr Carsley, the tenant of the flat upstairs, all breathless and in his shirt sleeves and braces.

'Miss Carmicheal, you need to get out, there's a fire at the factory, look! If that lot goes up…' He pointed in the direction of Silvertown and Amy could see a pall of smoke rising. The street was filling with people, rushing and shouting. She could hear the bells of the fire engines. She pulled her heavy brown working smock round her and locked the door behind her. Carsley began to run with the others away from the docks. She had no choice, her mother was there. She began running towards the works.

The Brunner Mond works in Crescent Wharf was on fire, and packed full with explosives. Panicking people were doing everything they could to get away from the smoke and its promise of Hell. There was a tide of ragged running women dragging ranting wretched children, going one way; and then sharply focussed policemen, anxious firemen and just Amy, trying to go the other way. She had reached the end of the street when a young policeman grabbed her and shook her.

'Get out, run for your life Miss; the whole bloody lot could go up!'

She managed to scream out: 'My mother…' then the explosion burst, lifting them both off their feet and hurling them into the air. The boom was deafening. She fell down on the pavement which was still shaking. There was the sound of glass shattering all around her. She had landed on her arm, but as yet the pain did not register. Glass and masonry began falling out of the sky on to her. The roof of the house behind her, splattered all around her on the pavement.

She lifted herself up, shielding her eyes from the falling debris. There were people lying all along the road, just like her. She saw the policeman, pick himself up and look around him then set off into the smashed and burning landscape. She tried to see what had happened to the factory but all she could see was the silhouettes of blackened broken buildings with a backdrop of burning bright orange flames.

Now red hot pieces of metal began raining down on to the streets and houses, the fire was spread by this storm. She half ran, half crawled into the porch of the house to find shelter, some cover from the burning. There was no air. She was struggling for breath. An orange glowing ember fell onto her heavy cotton smock and flamed there. She pushed it away with burning fingers. Then the world shook again.

Another explosion boomed, coming from across the river this time. A gas holder as far away as Greenwich had gone up. She watched a great blooming blue plume of fire rise up into the orange sky, the earth shook her angrily. With rising panic, she realised there was burning behind her now. As more rubble and embers and flames fell around her, she was forced to limp away from the place of shelter as it too, was now ablaze.

Keeping close to the burning terraces, to avoid the falling fire storm, she began making her way up the street, back to the flat. The smoke screen had fallen now and she coughed a hacking cough. All around her bemused people, dazed by the blast, stood and watched the awful splendour. It was a cold and wretched night, illuminated by some massive fireworks display. It seemed now that the whole city was on fire.

She found their flat. The windows were gone, the roof had caved in and sheets of flames now danced in her bedroom. As she watched the fire consume everything she owned, the heat burnt the side of her face. She turned her back on it and joined the throng of shocked people, walking away.

Again the human tide went in two directions. Ambulances and fire engines with bells ringing and men shouting were heading to the docks and the fires there; crowds of homeless refugees were wandering away, looking for streets where there were no flames. She cried as she stumbled with them through the gloom. The air was thick with acrid smoke. Most of the people were crying. A woman stumbled by her, sooty and black, hair smoking. She was just wearing a corset; her clothes had been blown away by the blast. In the rubble something loomed into focus that Amy would see and see again in her dreams. It was an arm, just an arm; a child's arm with a torn blue cotton bloody sleeve.

It was their factory that had gone up first, she was sure of that. Mother had stayed on to help with a shipment of 50 tons of T.N.T. that had just arrived at the Railway siding. Amy was sure she had gone. She could smell the T.N.T. in the air now, burning and falling around her.

Slowly she came to streets without burning. A policeman was rounding up the stricken, suffering people and ushering them in to a church. She wanted to walk on but he stopped her: 'This way Miss, First Aid Post here.' She wanted to push him away, but he took her arm and led her in. 'That arm needs seeing to Miss,' she had not been aware until then that she was injured. She looked down at her arm where she fell. Her smock was bloodstained round the elbow and as she saw it, she realised that she was in pain. Before, she had been too broken to notice.

Inside the church it was cool and light and quiet. She could hear the soft groans of people who were lying prostrate across the pews. A Nurse moved among them with bandages. Amy looked at the black cross, the pulpit, the list of hymn numbers to sing on Sunday; but in her mind she focussed only on her mother.

Time passed. Gradually the tide of human flotsam coming into the church ceased. People congregated together in small groups. The nurse bandaged Amy's arm and wrote down her name and address. They were brought tea and blankets. She knew no one there; she was totally, utterly alone. She cried until sleep overwhelmed her.

She woke early and her only thought was to get out and find her mother. She left the church quietly without waking the others. She began to walk back to the ruined terraces. There was nothing left of the flat but ash, burnt bricks and fallen rubble and so she began walking once more into Silvertown. Everywhere she went; there were men and women digging, scraping and operating machinery.

The fires were out now, but the barges on the river still poured water into the ruins. Familiar landmarks she passed on the way to work every morning were all destroyed, St Barnabas Church, the Primary School, the Fire Station, all just broken black shells, jutting out jaggedly from the rock strewn landscape. Just beyond them the police had established a cordon. She looked at the plain spreading down to the river, the plain of flattened burnt out rubble. Yesterday this had been an industrial landscape; there were warehouses, factories and sheds. Now you could see right down to the Thames. All ruined, all rubble, all gone. The soldiers at the roadblock would not let her pass. She explained her mother had been there and they looked at her with grim faces:

'The injured have been taken to the London Hospital Miss; you'll need to ask there for her. They are giving out Public assistance at Canning Town Public Hall Miss, later today. If you go there at two, you'll be helped to a place of safety. There's nothing left here.' As she walked she passed the car carrying the king and queen to visit the scene of London's biggest explosion.

Her journey from here to Hackett's farm was a long one. She buried her mother in Silvertown. She was paid compensation for her home. An Aunt put her up for a few weeks whilst she waited to join the Women's Land Army. The causes of the fire were never known, but the timing of it was merciful; an hour earlier and the factory would have been full, an hour later the people would have been lying upstairs, in rooms now completely destroyed. For a while it was rumoured to be a Zeppelin raid or an enemy arsonist, but the truth was less fanciful. It was an accident waiting to happen; the factory was originally built to make soda crystals. The owners thought it

123

too close to residential areas to turn it to munitions but the government insisted, and seventy people had died, four hundred were injured.

Amy promised herself and her mother's memory that from that point on in her life, she would never mill another shell and never again work in a factory. Her hair grew back blond and her arm healed. At last, she breathed again.

12.

Tuesday 10th August 1915 Perivale Camp, Middlesex

His mind shook him awake at 3am and he dressed by the light of the end of the night. He walked some distance through the darkness to where he had tethered the Harley against a tree, away from the tents. She was a noisy machine, you could hear her coming from a long way off and waking every chap in the camp at this time would not endear him to them. He untied the bike and kicked her into life. She started first time and he roared off down the lane and out on to the roads.

Clouds of dust blew up behind him as he leant the Harley into her first corner. He loved the deep bass notes of the engine. He liked achieving a fine balance on the machine, cranking her up more and more. The roads were clear at this time of day and he boomed through the night on her. It was a route he knew off by heart even in the dark which was just beginning to lift. He felt little wind on his face as he tore through the countryside, which was good. The planes he trained in would not go up if there was even a five mile an hour wind. He leant into a right curve and the Harley banked through it, then he straightened her up and banked, this time to the left and the bike curved with him, throwing up a dusty trail through the country road.

124

It was on a long route march down these very country roads when he'd come up with the idea of flying. Part of the decision came out of his frustration at still not being posted to France, despite transferring to the North Midlands Division of the Cyclist Corps. He'd joined the corps because he loved being on two wheels, and he thought them far more likely to be selected for active service, as they were a specialist unit. It had hurt to watch men he knew be sent to the front, while he still pedalled across fields and drilled every day. He had worked hard to prove himself a good officer and now he wanted to be a good pilot.

He pulled into Hendon aerodrome and made for the hangar, where the white painted letters showed that this was the RUFFY-BAUMANN FLYING SCHOOL. There were two planes outside the hangar this morning, both Maurice Farman Shorthorns. The boy was more used to the Longhorn, but another lad had taken that up yesterday and had a nasty smash in it, and so he would have to wait his turn to fly in the shorthorns that day. They called them 'Rumpetys' because that was how they flew.

He braked and pulled the back wheel of the bike round to a halt, stood it, and strode over to the hangar. The death of the bike's engine highlighted the silence of the airfield, the morning was beginning to squeeze in around him and the birds were beginning to sing. The promise of the sun was everywhere. Mechanics were already preparing the planes and Baumann was supervising them in a long leather flying coat. He greeted Ball:

'Ahh, the first Hun of the morning, Good Morning Sir, the man who would learn to fly must rise with the lark, isn't that right Lieutenant Ball?' They called the students Huns as they destroyed so many planes. Ball was an odd Hun.

125

'Morning Baumann, I should say so, although those dear fellows in my regiment won't allow me the time to fly at all, if I didn't follow the lark's daily routine. How's the Longhorn?'

Baumann shrugged, scrapes and smashes were the facts of life in any flying school. 'She needs a whole new top wing, it will take several days. The boy was back yesterday afternoon; wanted to know if he could still go up with a broken ankle. I sent him away with a flea in his ear for that one. How about taking me up this morning, just do a simple circuit and landing?' Ball nodded in agreement.

Flying helmets and goggles were put on and then the two men were helped to climb aboard the string bag that was the shorthorn. There were taut wires running everywhere, like spaghetti, across the wings. The two pilots sat in front of the wings giving a wide view from the nacelle, the round bucket with little red leather seats that they sat in. The plane was a pusher, the propeller span round behind you. You had to take special care not to let anything fall from the cockpit into the propeller which would be deadly. The trainer had dual controls, but Ball was to fly it. Baumann felt him taxi across the field and begin building up speed, then Ball pulled back on the joystick and the machine lifted into the sky. His take off had been okay, but his climb was slow and he took some time to gently bank the plane off to the right.

The sun was beginning to break free of the earth now and the light was good. The hours around dawn, when the wind was calmest, offered the best flying conditions. Baumann felt Ball was trying to fly her a little too quickly and made a mental note of it. Ball levelled the plane off and began his descent to the airfield. The speed was still too fast, which meant the ground was suddenly rushing up towards them. You really rode the air in these old planes, and felt every movement. Ball's ears and nose

126

felt as if they were bleeding; he slowed the machine down, but his stomach still felt like it was flying above him as he bumped her back to the ground. She bounced twice, before he could slow her and it was not, by any means, a pleasant landing. The sticks along the shorthorn's undercarriage were like skis and today's landing had felt much like a ski jump.

Baumann pulled his flying helmet off and looked at the boy:

'You know,' he said sneeringly, 'maybe you'd be better off taking your money and see if you can find a girl's flying school to enrol in, if that's how you are going to land a plane.'

Ball saw red:

'Thanks for the advice Sir, but I think you'll find I have had a total of fifteen minutes instruction on flying the shorthorn from Clarence Winchester, the first time I ever came to the aerodrome. I'll try again, if that's alright with you.'

His voice had risen and his eyes were fiery with temper. Baumann began climbing out of the cockpit,

'I think I'd prefer it if you did that solo Ball, take care of the machine.' He climbed down, helped by a mechanic and watched a grim faced Ball taxi away again.

Ball had gritted teeth as he pulled the shorthorn up into the sky for a second time. He was annoyed at himself mostly for misjudging his speed. Flying was something like a fast and furious fairground ride. You had no time to think, you had to really do it by feeling it. He had already had a fall and a terrible landing in the Longhorn, but he was utterly determined to show Baumann he could fly this thing. Flying was expensive, to get his aero club ticket which would get him into the Royal Flying Corps for a crack at getting his wings, was costing him £100. If he got the ticket first time, he'd get £60 back and he needed it. Although his Mess bills were low, he kept to himself; he had had few opportunities for making good deals recently to supplement his army salary.

He checked the speed, she was at sixty miles an hour now, which was better, he began the descent slower and the horizon rose more gently towards the field. He could see Baumann, standing, shading his eyes. The machine touched gently down this time, perfectly. He taxied across in front of Baumann and raised her up again, moving her across the field, ready again to take off. He felt inside the machine, with his hands he looked for all her little foibles. He used his hands to find her temperament and then caressed her accordingly. The wheels lifted and he soared into the dawn again.

Baumann had been reasonably impressed with the second landing. The boy was not a natural flyer, but knew no fear. Baumann had grown very used to this type of eager lad, who wanted to be able to fly all at once. They needed to learn their craft first, needed to put the time in. He liked Ball's pluck; he was here early and would come back again in the evening, after a day's work with his regiment. He also liked the fact that Ball wanted to know the entire machine. On days when it was too windy to fly the boy could be a real nuisance, he got in the way all the time and would not sit still. Baumann had discovered that if they gave him an engine and told him to take it to pieces and then told him to put it together again, it kept him quiet for hours.

Better that than the days he had brought his fiddle to the aerodrome. He had just started to learn the violin and one excruciating Saturday, two of the mechanics had threatened to resign or insert the violin into Ball, if he continued to make such a dreadful racket.

Ball brought the plane down to land for the third time and this time was perfect again. Baumann was relieved by this. He had not seen his temper before and Ball's fierceness had shocked him. He watched Ball taxi away and prepare for take off. Baumann realised he was making and double-underlining his point.

With this take-off, Ball felt comfortable and at ease enough with the plane to reach for the cake he had brought with him. Mother had sent a sponge cake which he had really enjoyed. He munched happily on it now. Flying had been a wonderful discovery for him, but it could be frightening at times. He was becoming used to the speed at which decisions had to be taken. He was beginning to enjoy the Shorthorn more and more. His family had been against him flying from the start. He had had to write and tell his mother not to keep writing about her fears of him crashing. The last one like that she'd written, he had of course, crashed. He landed the Rumpety again, this time the undercarriage stroked the ground. He pushed the kite back on her tiptoes to take off.

For Ball, flying was the highest height of the recent thrust of new technologies. The heavier than air flying machine was an extreme of Scientific and engineering achievements. It was no wonder older folks like his parents struggled to understand it and were afraid of it, but to an eighteen year old who found it entirely exhilarating, flying was the supreme moment of technology's ever speeding growth. Twelve years ago it was unthinkable, now it was his wonderful reality. Lol and Cill had driven down to see him fly the weekend before last, but there'd been a wind and he had only been able to show them some straights. They were younger; they understood the joys of it. This time he put the machine down almost with a flourish. He paused to check his watch before deciding he had time for just one more.

129

Pulling the stick back and moving towards take-off again he became aware that Baumann had stopped watching now and was doing something else. Albert had to be back to parade at Perivale at 6.45. He'd never been late, sometimes only managing a quick fifteen minute flight at Hendon before riding back. He had, however, been in trouble about the state of his uniform, it tended to get covered in oil from the plane and muck from the bike. So now he had to be back at 6.30 to change into a clean uniform for the day. They were going on an exercise that morning. He enjoyed those, running for cover with the other officers across the open ground.

His fifth and final landing was perfect. He extricated himself from the string bag, waved triumphantly to Baumann, ran across the aerodrome, jumped on the Harley and roared off into the morning under the deep bass boom of the engine.

Thursday March 29th 1917 London Colney Aerodrome

He played it with nervous energy; he went just a little too fast. He fiddled frantically for them, the bow twitching in his hands and he smiling. They clapped in time then had to speed up as he did. He whirled as he played in the pool of bright red light. He had lit a flare to serenade her by. Now she and Bill sat clapping on the edge of his light. He swooped to his finale and the bow pulled a final rasping note out of the violin, and then bowed low and flamboyantly to their cheers.

He put the violin down and picked up a book she had given him. It lay next to the big black Lewis gun that had been his preoccupation for the day. That and avoiding the other officers, he was being ribbed mercilessly because of Flora.

'Read me one last one, and then I think you'd better get young Bill back to bed Bobs.' He gave her the slim red leather volume and she flicked through it until she found the one that pleased her. She read from the red light of the flare, her voice was soft and rang out over the flare's quiet hiss.

'My Wife

Trusty, dusky, vivid, true,

With eyes of gold and bramble-dew,

Steel-true and blade-straight,

The great artificer

Made my mate.'

The flare spluttered and died. He took a hurricane lamp from beside the gun and brought it close so she could continue. The shadows flickered around them. He thought her voice lovely, it had a musical tone:

'Honour, Anger, Valour, fire:

A love that life could never tire.

Death quench or evil stir,

The mighty master

Gave to her.

Teacher, tender comrade, wife.

A fellow-farer true through life'

Heart-whole and soul free

The august father

Gave to me.'

'That's lovely' he said, 'I like that one best of all.'

She smiled, 'You said that about Requiem as well.'

'Well, I like that one but in a different way, this one's best I think.'

131

'I should read them in a Scottish accent; Louis-Stephenson was a proper Scot.'

He wouldn't hear of it. 'Your accent is just right for it Bobs, you should put it to music and sing it to me.'

She had arrived to pick him up in the evening. He had made a special effort. He had been working all day on the Lewis gun. Life often depended on the thing moving smoothly, which it rarely seemed to do. He was always careful to rack up the drums of ammunition the right way. He would spend hours on it, and the gun still jammed. Today he had been holding the great black metal thing all day, greasing and degreasing it. Checking every mechanism, repeating click after click to check the sound was clean. This was the thing that had won him his medals, it was his gun. It needed cherishing.

Working with the gun was greasy, oily work, so he had stopped early for once and got changed. He wanted to make an effort this time and be smart. He knew Rhys-Davies or Lewis or any of the others would pounce on him if they saw him like that, and so then he had hidden away round the base waiting for her. She looked so fine when she got there. She'd changed already, managing to get out of an evening's milking. She wore a straw hat which framed her face with bright yellow flowers. He thought it quite charming.

They'd met Bill at the Peahen in St Albans. They had dinner there, under the low beams and by candlelight. There was blackout because of the Zeppelin raids. They'd eaten a pie which he pronounced 'topping' and the waitress had blushed at his compliments. She'd stared at his medal ribbons when he first got there. Flora tended to forget that he was a celebrity until such moments as these reminded her. He never liked to talk about what he did, the thing that made him famous, but she'd pressed him that night.

She'd pretended she was giving Albert the chance to impress Bill, but she wanted to know for herself. Being up there with him had been one thing, but being up there and fighting; she had avoided imagining it. He'd talked very quietly and with a hushed intensity:

'What's it like when you fight up there?' She asked outright. There was a pause where she thought she should never have asked and he fought somewhere inside himself for the words. Bill leant forward eagerly, this he wanted to hear.

'I flew BE2s at first to take photographs. They were slow sitting targets. A lot of very brave men have died in those; a lot of better men than me. I fly scouts now, single seat jobs. They are quicker. That means everything, everything happens so quickly when you are in a scrap. Sometimes you are flying along and bullet holes appear by magic in your wings. They say you never see the one that gets you and I believe it.'

'Tell us about one of your fights Albert.' Bill was being direct now. Worry clouds crossed over Albert's face, and then he retrieved something and looked comfortable. 'Last Summer I had one ripping scrap with a Hun. He was in a Two-seater, a Roland I think, and I was in my Nieuport. He came at me head-on at first, so I knew he had plenty of nerve. We swooped round each other, taking it in turns to get behind and fire off a few rounds into the other's tail. Neither of us could quite get the upper hand, but I had hit his Observer I think. I was coming in to finish him off when the gun just lamely clicked in my hand. I was out of ammunition; I'd used all three drums. I took my pistol from my holster and tried to get alongside him. We pointed

133

revolvers at each other and fired. Neither gun worked. We laughed; I could see his face quite clearly. He waved and then flew off. He was clearly a good sport and he knew how to fly that plane well. Not all of them are like that.'

Bill was wide eyed: 'Is it true that they run off as soon as they see your red spinner coming?' Flora looked at him, 'Really Bill, you should not believe everything you read in the 'Evening Standard.' Albert was unperturbed.

'They have been known to, yes. Most of them don't want to fight at all.'

She had brought the book out of her bag then; they had talked as much as she could bear about fighting. He had been delighted and embarrassed. He made lots of promises over what gift he would give her in return. He'd held the slim volume and told her he would keep it near him when in France. He asked her to read one to him then and he'd chosen Requiem:

This be the verse you grave for me:

Here he lies, where he longed to be:

Home is the sailor, home from the sea,

  And the hunter home from the hill.'

'Where he longed to be' she repeated, 'Oh it's too sad, why did he long to be there?' Albert flashed dark eyes at her, and then looked down.

'He doesn't long to be there, he longs to do his duty, he'd rather come home with the hunter.'

'You must come home.' She had said it without thinking; it was a truth that hit her. The table spun and Bill and the rest of the room were there no longer, just his eyes.

'I will.' He said, and she took that as a promise and held on to it fiercely through many dark nights.

She drove him back to the aerodrome and he put on the show for her. His gun brooded over them, she was aware of it all the time. Bill looked at it admiringly. She thought it an ugly black thing.

Albert promised to fly out to the farm again the next day. She said she'd listen for the engine. Bill got into the car first and looked away. Albert had the chance to kiss her. He stood holding her hand, flushed and coughed.

'Good night Bobs' and he retreated back out of the light.

She leapt into the car, made the engine roar and drove furiously away

13.
Monday May 7th 1917 Vert Galant Aerodrome.

Maxwell felt decidedly edgy. He had the least flying time in an SE5 of any man in the squadron. It had been his choice, he could blame no one else, but now his lack of experience just might be found out. The skies above France were a pretty unforgiving place. He had been 'discovered' by Ball when Blomfield was putting the squadron together. Ball had done the round of training squadrons and decided that he and Barlow would make perfect Scout pilots. As the squadron was forming, he had taken a single flight in a new SE5 – the RFC were treating their new weapons like diamonds then. What he hadn't expected was the fast speed of the machine on landing; his first landing back in March had been poor, he'd nearly overshot. So he had avoided the planes for a while. When they reached France he'd clocked up a total of twenty two minutes flying time. Since then, they'd patrolled every day when the planes had finally all been converted to Blomfield's liking. He'd been in plenty of scraps and had a few nasty scrapes.

There were two ways of looking at being in 'A' flight. You could see only the positives; they were all fine airmen and could wish for no better flight commander than Ball. Their flight commander was the highest scoring pilot on the allied side, you could ask for no finer example. The flight had also all managed to gain at least one victory since the work began. Maxwell had bagged his first Hun when on patrol with Knight two weeks earlier. The negative side of flying behind Ball was his rashness. He was never really a formation flyer, he preferred to go up and hunt alone. He had the instincts of a lone hunter and if you followed him, you had to be prepared for that. There could come a moment when he would see an aircraft you had no idea was there. He would fire a Very light to let you know then go off on some steep climb, dive or turn, expecting you to follow. This was not always the easiest of tasks.

Maxwell had been made distinctly edgier by his 'bump' a week or so before. Whilst patrolling with Ball, Maxwell had got into a scrap and his controls had been shot away. He had a desperate time trying to nurse the falling machine back to the lines. He managed to get as far as the mud filled shell craters around Combles. He had tried to put her down neatly but could not control the speed. The wings were torn from the plane and the detached fuselage bounced along the craters, with him still trapped inside it. He had rolled along the ground with the wind continually being knocked out of him, and then crawled out totally dazed and unsure where he was, until a nearby Tommy came over to help him. He walked away alive but not knowing how. He had nightmares about it for three nights after it happened.

You had to like the boy Ball. He was completely focussed on the job, always up to his armpits in oil, taking apart some instrument or other. He left nothing to chance, personally checking every detail of his plane and gun's performance. Maxwell had learnt a lot from him. Ball never wore goggles or a flying helmet; he had led the flight over to France bare-headed. Maxwell found this hard to understand. It got so cold flying at altitude. Sometimes your whole body seemed to freeze from the waist downwards, even in summer. If you put your hand out of the cockpit for any length of time, frostbite was the most likely result.

Maxwell had spent the morning carefully filling his ammunition drums for the Lewis gun to prevent a jam later. The worst thing, in his opinion, about the SE5 was the need to change ammunition drums on the Lewis, in mid-flight; often, in mid-combat. His gun had so far, not jammed at a vital moment, but almost every pilot in the squadron could recount a time when theirs had. Now he was greasing the mounting, making sure that when needed, the gun would swing easily down into his arms. He looked over to Ball's plane and saw him performing the same task, as was the third of their flight, Lieutenant Kenneth Knaggs. Then Ball attached a tiny black cat mascot under the wings, they were all so superstitious in the service, because death fiercely courted them.

137

'A' flight had the most kills between them in the squadron at this point and Maxwell felt that this was due to the extensive preparations which Ball made them put in for every patrol. Their riggers and fitters had become used to the abominable state of Ball's plane every time he returned from the air. They used to guess at the number of bullet holes his machine would be peppered with. He never disappointed them.

The three pilots came together next to Ball's plane so he could go through their orders. Flight briefings were brief of necessity, Ball's the briefest. Normally Blomfield liked to be with them for this, but he was away at Savy so Ball explained what their orders were:

'We are to meet up with Sopwiths from 70 squadron. They are on artillery reconnaissance duties. We rendezvous at 9000 feet. We are to lead and escort them over to take photos between Caudry and Neuvilly. Should we see any Huns, then I intend shooting them down. If I break off, stay and cover the Strutters.' The three men rubbed Vaseline from a shared pot into the exposed skin on their faces.

Knaggs looked into the sky:

'There are some thicker clouds forming, and they're getting lower.'

Clouds made you apprehensive, they provided you with cover, but you could lose your horizons and they could hide the Huns all day.

Ball was decisive:

'If they get any thicker or lower, I will adjust our height to keep us out of it.' He studied the air. 'I think it will stay fine enough for the rest of the afternoon. Keep a look out for albartri, especially the red ones.'

The patrol was the routine stuff of the RFC. You could argue that the Corps' sole true purpose was to take photographs of the German artillery. The scouts were just a sideshow. Maxwell felt a certain respect for the pilots who took to the skies daily in

out of date obsolete Sopwiths and BE2s; they had neither the speed nor the armaments

that the scout planes had. Without their escort, they were an easy target for the Red

Baron and his like.

Maxwell climbed back into his cockpit and checked all the levels for a final time.

She started first time and he followed Ball's brown plane across the field. The three

planes went up on their tiptoes then climbed into the sky. Maxwell began checking

all his levels again, the readings were good and she was running smoothly. Cold air

rushed by him as he made his steady climb up into the blue. There were some clouds

floating by, but the day was good for flying. He looked all around him as he flew.

There were unlikely to be Hun kites at this level, they rarely flew over the lines, but

Ball would see them first if they did come this far, then you could be sure of a scrap.

Maxwell's path to being a pilot was via Gallipoli. He had enrolled in the Infantry,

had been made an officer and sent to take part in the landings at Suvla bay. It had

been an interesting introduction to war; the smell of burning bodies, the constant

artillery fire booming overhead, the dead, lying in piles, the heat, the blood, the lice.

The allies had completely underestimated the Turkish soldier and he had made them

pay dearly for it. They were bogged down on hillsides with nothing but scrubland for

cover. So many young men had lost their lives on that Peninsula. For months, he had

grown used to coming under shellfire even when he bathed in the sea. You were

exposed to fire the whole time you were there. He had met 56th Squadron's

Recording Officer, 'Grandpa' Marson there, just before it was decided that the

Dardanelles were a sideshow and had to be abandoned. The campaign had cost

Marson a leg. Maxwell was luckier; he had got away still whole, at least physically.

There were days, even now when he remembered waking up in a scrawny tent clinging to a Turkish hillside. He still heard the artillery booming through the night.

They rendezvoused with the big brown lumbering Sopwiths of 70 Squadron at 9000 feet. Ball led his flight straight to them without a map. He knew these skies as if they were his own. Then the SE5s led them to the east and over the lines. A few clouds of bursting Archie had exploded inaccurately thousands of feet beneath them. The slower speed of the two seat planes meant that Ball's flight had to fly pretty sluggishly along the way. There did not seem to be another aircraft in the sky. Ball's red nosecone often did that. The Huns would see who it was in their airspace and decide to take a day off.

They waited above the Sopwiths while the machines lumbered along in straight lines, photographing all the terrain. Ball circled, ever-anxious for combat but apart from a single solitary two seat Hun machine which turned tail and ran over Beauvois, they seemed alone in the sky. Then there was the burst of a red flare from Ball's plane. He signalled to Maxwell and Knaggs to stay over the Sopwiths and cover them, their photos would be vital to the war effort. He dived down beneath them. From above Maxwell could see where Ball's dive was intended to end. Underneath him, a mixed bag of albartri and two seater hun machines had appeared. Maxwell could see Ball's guns blazing, even now cutting into the fuselage of the Albatross beneath him. Then the firing ceased, the gun must have jammed again. The relieved Albatross set off with his companions to get out of range of the attacking machine. Ball rose back up to rejoin his flight.

The Sopwiths below had begun flying away to the East, their work finished for the day. The flight remained above them. Maxwell could still see the German kites,

140

some way off to the East. They did not seem anxious to tackle the red spinner again. Maxwell imagined Ball taunting them, shaking his fists and appealing for them to come nearer. He had watched Ball clear his jammed gun and prepare to fight again. He could feel his Flight Commander's impatience. His every instinct would be straining to roar off after the enemy aircraft that still followed them, albeit at a safe distance, but as commander, it was Ball's duty to stay with his formation that had a duty to remain with the Sopwiths, and their precious cargoes of photographs.

As they made their way back, he could see Ball staring the whole time in his mirror. Ball flew slower and slower, almost pleading with the Hun patrol to catch up with them, to join the fight. His desire to attack was a tangible thing. Then he signalled to Maxwell to stay with the other planes. He banked off to the left, dived at speed and headed back. The Huns must have seen him because that was the moment they chose to disappear. Ball circled for a few minutes before rejoining their flight back over the lines.

The observer in the final Sopwith waved as they slipped away to their aerodrome and Maxwell returned the wave. He followed Ball down towards the Vert Galant, the landing was always the part which made him most nervous. You had to get her down to around 50mph and her stalling speed was only 42. It left little room for error. His mouth was dry but his hands stayed steady. He knew Blomfield would be back by now and be watching. He always commented on how well you landed. If Maxwell misjudged it, his usual tactic was to let it bounce once, then give her more engine, effectively taking off again before making another approach. He watched Ball put his machine down perfectly. He levelled his own machine off when the altimeter showed 20 feet then dropped her down and her wheels rolled across the field smoothly. He knew he could face Blomfield with his head held high. He climbed down from the cockpit and made his way to Marson's hut to hand in his report. The clouds that blew over the aerodrome now were thick and grey and full of storms.

Monday May 7th 1917. Hackett's Farm.

Amy put all the power she could muster into the swing of the axe, but the ring against the bark made no impact. The axe bounced hopelessly way and hung limp in her arms. She breathed deeply and turned to the other girls.

'It's no use, after all that digging, I've had it. We'll never get this one down.' She wiped her palm on the trunk of the broad oak. They had been taking trees from the wood ever since they came to the farm. Wood was always urgently needed to make limber and ammunition boxes and all the other things that now lined the way between the farm and France. Evidence of the girls' previous efforts were all around them in the form of newly cut trees and neatly piled logs but this old oak was proving to be a tough one.

  Flora stepped forward next and took the axe from Amy. The air was rich with drizzle that glistened on the axe. She swung it hard into the side of the tree and it sliced into the bark. She breathed heavily and Beatrice stood opposite her, axe poised. Her blade cut deeply into the wood. They managed to work in tandem for six or eight strokes but each time the axe cuts seemed to get smaller and the trunk of the tree grew impossibly wider. Flora signalled a pause to Beatrice and they stepped back to turn and pant. They were giggling now, their own struggles with the more demanding tasks of the day were often a joke they shared.

142

Violet stepped forward. She took Flora's place and Amy, renewed now, took over from Beatrice. Violet smiled:

'Now we'll see her tumble. Come on Amy lets count them off. One.'

Her axe tore into the white flesh of the exposed tree.

'Two', Amy brought the axe home this time, stroke after stroke bit into the wood.

Violet tensed her shoulders to bring the axe home

'Three, you nasty, German tree.' At this, Amy collapsed with laughter, the momentum gone. They had developed this game in the woods many times. The tree to be felled was always a German, except once when Violet had decided it was a Turk with a big black moustache. The idea was to give them the strength to get the things down and then cut into logs. It was hard physical work and the games helped pass the time, but this one frequently had them collapsing with giggles.

For Violet the laughter was only partly irony. Sometimes she found real strength in the game; she could imagine it really was a German. For once, she could fight back at what had happened to her. She had seen too much and carried too much with her still. She wondered if these things could ever leave her. The farm for her was a respite, at least for some of the time.

The loss that hurt the most was not the first one she had suffered. Both her parents were dead by the time she joined her local Voluntary Aid Detachment in Aldershot. She became a VAD girl, a volunteer nurse. When she told Ralph, her brother, of her intentions, he had laughed and told her she would 'fall in love with the first well heeled Tommy with a Blighty that came along.' He had been right, that was the bitter part of the joke. Technically Ted's was the first wound that she had dressed.

143

She'd found nursing so draining and not at all what she thought it would be. She wore long grey starched robes; it was like being a nun. Her job appeared to be scrubbing things with cold water and carbolic soap. She'd been doing it for months, scrubbing floors, stone steps, tables, wheelchairs and walls. She emptied bed pans and handed out meals. She'd imagined being a white robed angel behind the British lines, mopping fevered brows of strong wounded men. In fact, it had been a camp hospital in Aldershot, a bucket and a scrubbing brush. She'd tried not to moan but it had been hard.

There had been an exercise in the camp and something had gone wrong with a gun, a big artillery piece had exploded. The normally quiet hospital had filled in an hour and even Violet had been called to the emergency ward. It was lined with men on stretchers. Violet was handed a bandage and told to help with the seated wounded. She'd only ever put a bandage on a dummy before, and so she chose her man carefully. It was shrapnel wound to the shoulder; she'd practiced shoulder wounds before.

She was very gentle with him, my, but he was tall. He wasn't English, his voice had a twang. He told her he was fine and it was just a scratch. He had asked her name. His height had surprised her when he stood. He had a shock of blond hair and blue eyes. She noticed he was an Officer and he smiled a row of bright white teeth at her. She'd moved on to another man and he'd continue to wait his turn.

He was waiting for her when her shift finished hours later. He asked to walk her back to the Nurses home and she walked with him, although she did explain that strictly speaking it was not allowed. He was from Newfoundland. She had never heard a more romantic place name and liked to say it. He was Second Lieutenant

Edward Manning of the First Newfoundland Regiment, Ted. He was Ted. He was this sudden force in her life. They only met three times before he was posted overseas, but his letters came every day and with them came hope; hope of a new life on a farm in the peace and green of Newfoundland. Ted had told her often she would never see anywhere more beautiful.

Nursing became more involved than the cleaning it had entailed up until now. She applied to go overseas. Ted had encouraged her. He sent her postcards and words and pictures. Each letter seemed to pull them closer. They shared the things they liked, made dreams, built houses. She found poems and cuttings for him. She had placed a picture she had found of Newfoundland by her bed. It was snowy, which she had not imagined. His letters became a pulse for her. Some days they were the only evidence she was alive at all.

She was sent to a Hospital at Calais. She had to learn on her feet. Casualties came in daily and she was for a while the first one to lift the blankets and recommend where they were taken. It happened like a dream for her, the line-ups of stretchers, and the boys underneath them cut up like meat, the morphine injections, and the constant cry for water. She still scrubbed and cleaned, every day; but now it was usually bodies of young boys. The orderlies were men too bad or mad to become soldiers, so they dropped the boys and just left them. She cajoled and sometimes forced them to take the boys to the right place.

She had seen some grisly wounds. The ones with parts of their faces burnt or blown away were the worst to some people but she had learnt to loathe the stumps. She had to bathe stumps which had once been arms or legs, some gangrenous, some that stank. The war was turning men to mincemeat; so much torn flesh had passed before her.

145

Gas attacks had also come in to the hospital, rows of blinded men drowning in their own bodily fluids.

All this and she had fleas, they had embedded themselves in the hems of her skirts and she constantly itched, even after a bath. She shared a Nissen hut with several women who snored loudly and one that refused to wash. One night they had all screamed at a rat in the hut until she killed it with her shoe. She spent hours at the hospital in the evenings, turning off the lights, waiting for the cockroaches to come out and then stamping on them. She washed blood and pus from stone floors. She watched men die; fit, young, healthy Englishmen, Australians, Canadians. Destroyed by machine guns or shattered by shells, they died.

There was one night when a boy she had liked and they thought was getting better just went. They had promised him that he would be well enough to walk next day but he had a bad head wound; part of his brain had been shot away. He had spoken to her quite lucidly at dinner, then his mouth was foaming at supper, then he was dead.

And she could bear no more, not one more day. She could not see another broken body. No more, she had told herself, no more. Then he came.

Ted was there, it was the summer of 1916 and the hospital was at a lull for a change, maybe because the big push was due. He just walked into the ward where she was working. She was holding a bottle of warm urine when she saw him. He was just there, no build up, nothing.

He was older and broader she saw at once. She put the bottle down and went to him. She was not aware that she was sobbing, until she tried to speak. She buried her head in his chest and cried. He was there; he had come marching through the mists for her. For her, he had risen from the trenches and crossed no-mans land. No machine gun could stop him, he floated over the wire; for her, all this for her. She looked up at him through tears; he was so strong, outlined by the sunlight.

The matron was beside herself at his appearance. Her nurses would not, could not, must not fraternise with the men. He suddenly became her brother, that quietened the anguish, but they were never left alone. He saw her twice that summer and then he went away. She still had to go home. She saw the men in her dreams. She focussed on the parts of them the war had taken away. She saw blood and stumps, they refused to leave her.

Unlike the poor men, she could go and she would go home. Home to wash and breathe again, home to let the nightmares fade, home to receive the telegram that told her he had finally been taken away. Without his letters, she had died. The life had ebbed out of her and just when she thought it might get better, she had received the letter that told her that Ralph had died on the same day. It had left her bereft and alone in the world.

Now her axe bit meanly into the tree, and the great oak swayed. She lunged her hob nailed boot at it with a fierce kick and it quivered. Flora called out:

'Violet, look out, the cow!' And the great oak broke and fell to the ground with a crash that echoed and echoed around the broken wood.

14.

Friday September 15th 1916. The skies above Bapaume, France

Good things and bad news came in threes. He had learnt that a long time ago. This was his third sortie of the day in his third different plane. Below him the Somme battle was entering its third phase. He had three white tailed Le Prieur rockets attached to each wing of his Nieuport and he was looking for his third victory of the day. Although he still wasn't quite sure if he could claim the second one; the Lewis gun had cracked him on the head at a critical moment. He'd lost consciousness whilst firing on a Hun. He still had a vague headache even now.

Boom Trenchard had told them to expect to be busy. Albert had seen why with his own eyes that day. The noise of their aeroplanes was being used to hide the noise of the tanks. The great lumbering things had gone over that morning. They were supposed to be able to cross barbed wire and trenches, they spurted machine gun fire from each side. The shock of their slow tortuous crossing of No mans land must have scared the fight out of the Huns. Albert had noticed that a number had not made the crossing, they lay silent in the field, some had been wrecked, but he had reported back that he had seen a group of nine trundle through the melting snow up to the German front trench, raking its occupants with streams of fire. They were great green man-eating diamonds that stalked so slowly; from the air they were just toys. The Generals were hoping these were the toys that would win the war. For the men that rolled inside their hot and stifling metal bowels, their games were hard to play.

Boom Trenchard had been to ask for volunteers to go balloon bursting the day before. The Huns had lined the tanks' jump off point with observation balloons. There had been a special meeting in the mess at Bellevue; somewhere Albert rarely visited these days. He preferred spending time in his tent listening to the gramophone or playing the fiddle. Boom had congratulated them all on their work and explained that the observation balloons needed downing before the morning's attack. As commander of 'A' flight, Lieutenant Ball's was the first hand raised.

148

Boom already knew Ball from the 'spy' mission Ball had undertaken the previous year. Ball had wanted to attract attention. He wanted to fight in Scouts, not observe in BE2s, so he had volunteered to drop a spy behind the enemy lines. The mission was undertaken at night; there was a lot of Archie bursting around them, flashes of it were continually lighting the air. They had no gun as they had to carry the spy's luggage. Things were too hot and the spy, Victor, refused to leave the plane. He said that he would be shot. Albert had landed four times, each at a more isolated spot and still Victor had refused to budge. Ball flew home furiously annoyed but Boom was pleased. He sent ball a letter full of thanks and praise which Ball sent home to his father. The flights in single seat scouts were forthcoming.

All the officers thought Boom a fine man to fly for. He had shaken Ball's hand warmly while he explained the mission to Ball, Major Smith-Barry and Lieutenant Walters who would be flying it alongside him. Boom was a tall man with a booming voice and imposing manner, but he clearly understood the work the boys did in the air. He pointed out to them on the map the exact location of the balloons. The rockets would bring them down, but they also took Buckingham ammunition. These allowed you to follow the bullets' burning trail across the sky. If the rockets missed the bullets would ignite the gas filled balloons.

The day had started so brightly. He had been given official notification that he had been awarded the Russian Order of St George Fourth Class. Another reward for his efforts, he already had a Military Cross and two days before had been awarded a bar for his Distinguished Service Order, the first man in the war to receive this. He always liked the fact that his mother was so proud of the medals that he wore. That meant a lot to Albert. He saw his medals as rewards given to him for a job well done, and looked forward to adding a Victoria Cross one day, if he made it.

Balls and Walters took their planes over Bapaume just after ten that morning, but the balloons had all been taken down before they could reach them. They had circled in frustration for a time and then Ball's keen eyes had spotted a German bi-plane beneath them. He dived down on it with his chest tight and his teeth gritted. He threw the switch to fire his rockets and they hissed away from him menacingly leaving a trail of white fire behind them.

The Hun tilted first to the left, then to the right to avoid the burning rockets. Ball followed them and got under the startled German, raking his underside with the tearing Buckingham bullets he could see bursting through the fabric of the plane. The German spun wildly out of control and fell from the sky. Ball soared his plane higher and watched Walters following his lead. He scored a direct hit with one of his rockets on a LVG which caught fire and soon became a burning wreck below them.

Ball wanted more. The rockets made great sport. As he flew A212 at three that afternoon and got hit on the head by his Lewis whilst bringing down an albatross; his mechanics loaded more rockets on to A201. They had to rig the plane as he liked it, they made it tail-heavy. That made it fly itself easier when he was firing; it gave him a stable gun platform. He'd kept his own gun with him in each plane as he had spent a long time at the target butts the day before harmonising its range to exactly sixty feet; his perfect attacking distance. He also made sure his mechanics would fit A201 with his red spinner. That seemed to clear the skies some days on its own.

Now as it whirled in front of him, flying at 3,000 feet he saw three cream fat Rolands below him; the inevitable three. They were circling, waiting, and becoming prey for him. He pulled down the Lewis and dived. The air flew past him and his heart flew into his dry mouth. His finger pushed the button and the rockets shot away leaving their white trails for him to follow through the skies. The shocked Huns jumped to avoid them; these were not a weapon they had seen before. His hands grasped the Lewis and squeezed breathlessly. He got right under the middle plane, the other two dived away in panic and he fired and fired and the gun rattled for him spitting fire all over the belly of the Hun machine. Tiny holes were bursting just beneath the petrol tank. The great fish fell; spinning and crashing down, falling in spirals to earth and dying.

His job done, he turned back towards Bellevue as the sun began its downward journey.

Thursday April 5th 1917 Shenley

His hands were clutching the altar rail and his eyes were closed. He murmured prayers deeply. He was deep within himself, finding the God that protected him. He was wearing a plain black suit and civilian shoes, underneath his overcoat. He wanted no recognition here, he wanted the answer to his question and there was a voice that he needed to hear. The golden identity bracelet he wore tapped lightly against the polished wooden rail. Oh that his Father would give him an answer.

It was Holy Thursday. They were leaving for France on Saturday; he had just two nights left with her. The church service had been a time of quiet contemplation for him. There were just a dozen in the congregation in the little chapel and now just the caretaker and the priest remained as he completed this personal devotion. They shook

151

his hand warmly as he left. There had been an answer, one he really knew already. This night he would tell her.

He'd spent the weekend with his parents in Nottingham once the expected mobilisation of the squadron had come through. He'd flown out to the farm twice more and the second time he'd been spotted. A paragraph had appeared in the Evening Standard calling him a flying Romeo. He vaguely suspected that one of the other girls on the farm had tipped the paper off. He liked being thought of as a hero, but hated the fuss that went with it. Life in the Mess had been hell once he'd been given the flying Romeo tag. Lewis had even acted out the balcony scene from an upper window for them all.

His mother had been full of questions for him about Flora; in fact he'd spent the whole weekend avoiding the subject with his family. They could see the change in him, the fire in his eyes. Whilst at Sedgeley, a little girl had come to the house, a neighbour's child. She had given him a lucky black cat mascot and he'd promised to attach it to his plane. He'd tidied his things away, wrapping his letters with red ribbons. There had been finality about the way everything had been left, that was born of some distant foreboding. It felt like every thing he did, he was doing for the final time.

He waited for her car by the road. It was a cold night for April and a single flake of snow floated past him. He walked over to the pub by the pond. Three ducks idly floated on the pond's black waters. He stood next to the tiny cage there watching them. The eighteenth century cage was an odd little white thimble that stood next to Shenley duck pond. Years ago it was used to keep the village miscreants in a safe place before carting them off to Barnet to appear before the bench. It had two little black barred windows. One was inscribed with 'Be sober, be vigilant', the other said 'Do well and fear naught.' It was just big enough inside for two people to stand there.

She was wearing the brooch he had bought her when she arrived. It was an RFC officer's wings, cut in fine diamonds. It sparkled in the lights from the pubs warm windows, a tiny beautiful thing. He had bought it from jewellers in Nottingham and had hidden it away from prying parents.

He beckoned her out of the car and she joined him. They stood in the darkness as he opened the outer door of the cage and then the inner one. She still hadn't spoken as he grasped her hand and pulled her inside. They were close in the darkness of the little white cage and just a little light came in through the barred windows. He reached out and she felt the warmth of his hand on the back of her neck and finally, his lips met hers and he kissed her, gently at first, then as she responded, there was a longing in his kiss that they both knew well now. He tried to pull back but she still held him close.

At last they stood apart again and he spoke:

'You can never know how many times I wanted to do that, but was afraid to be forward, you do realise I love you, don't you Bobs? You must have known it.'

He could see her lips form a smile in the darkness. He looked deeply at her. She asked, full of longing:

'Am I really so terrifying? I would never have stopped you kissing me.'

He breathed again and his breath was as fog in the darkness.

'No, but supposing you said no and pushed me away, what would I do then?'

'I will never say No to you.' And she meant it.

They drove much of the way back to St Albans in silence. There was a new intimacy between them that was warm and real. He told her about the squadron's preparation for flying away on Saturday. He asked her not to come to the aerodrome that day. He hated cold goodbyes like that. She reminded him he had promised to let Bill see the squadron take off.

Mother had made a pie for him and he ate with relish back at her house. Bill wanted to know all about his work on the plane and he told them all about the mechanics and riggers that helped him. He was becoming more at ease with her family now. Albert wanted her to sing again but she declined and promised a performance tomorrow night.

He wished Bill a fond Cheer O and she drove him back to the aerodrome. He was quiet at first then he started falteringly.

'I have been thinking and praying about this and I think it best that I give you this.' She was watching the dark road carefully as he took off his gold identity bracelet and placed it around her wrist at the wheel. It was a tiny delicate thing, she could see. Then he continued, 'I think we should be married as soon as the war is over. I want this to be your engagement ring'

The shock of it nearly made her turn into a ditch. She skidded the car to a halt and sat there open mouthed. 'Yes', she heard herself saying.

15.

Monday February 19th 1917. Sedgeley House.

The Oldsmobile's white tyres swirled in the gravel drive as Albert pulled up. He parked next to Lol's car and was met by Goff, the family collie bounding up, tail wagging and his father's firm handshake.

'Hey up Lad, your mother will be pleased to see you; she thought you might cry off.'

'Cheer O father, have you been banished from the house again?'

'I am partaking in a cigar out here at your mother's request. She has a new hat and frock and does not want to go to your ceremony smelling of my cigars. How was your journey down? This looks a little beauty.' He ran a gloved hand along the side of the black Oldsmobile.

'She belongs to an instructor at the base, I was thinking of buying one so he lent it to me for a day or two. She drives well.'

His father studied him for a moment. 'So, that thousand's burning a hole in your pocket is it?' Albert had been paid a thousand pounds just before Christmas by a leading aircraft manufacturer. It was to retain his services at the end of the war. His

father felt that Albert had accepted the money, but had no intention of taking the job.

'No, it's not that, I just want Lol to be jealous.' He smiled. Mother knocked on the

window and beckoned them in. They exchanged hugs in the parlour and Albert sat

down next to her on the long red sofa.

'It's so good to have you home at last, my boy.' Harriet had been looking forward to

the day for a long time. He had been dreading it and had made no secret of the fact.

'It's good to be home mother.' The maid brought tea and they drank a cup together.

He told them all his news.

It had been a bad winter for him. He had arrived home back in Nottingham in

October and suddenly found himself a celebrity after reaching a total of 30 victories,

and then the powers that be had decided it was better to keep him at home. He was

good for morale, this war lacked heroes, living ones that was. He had been given a

succession of meaningless postings as an instructor, teaching raw recruits to fly. He

yearned for combat as soon as he felt rested.

He and father had begun their campaign to get him back to the front by writing to the

Director of Air Organisation, Brigadier-General Charlton DSO. Then Father had a

quiet word with his friend Duckham at the Munitions ministry, but still had no joy.

They had then tried the combination of Mr Richardson, MP for Melton, Jimmy White,

the financier and the Press Baron, Lord Northcliffe. At one point, Albert Senior

worried that the boy had upset Northcliffe. The Lad had promised to take his mother

to the Nottingham Empire for dinner but Northcliffe had phoned inviting him to

dinner the same day. Albert had turned him down.

'Perhaps you were unwise,' vouched his Father, 'He might be a good deal of use to you.' The boy was annoyed.

'I'm surprised at you,' he growled. 'I don't want any help. Isn't my mother more important than anyone else? I have promised to take her to the Empire and no one on earth could stop me.'

Northcliffe's help however, was what had got him the posting to his new squadron and ultimately, back to France. He was to join the 56th Squadron at London Colney next week. They were a scout squadron and Albert knew he would soon be back at the front in a single seat scout. His father had asked him if he went back, was he certain he'd get through it. The boy said:

'No scout pilot who does any serious fighting, and sticks it for any time, can get through.' His father baulked at this.

Now mother handed him a magazine. It had a picture of the three of them and Lol standing in front of Sedgeley. 'Home after a hundred fights' was the caption. He laughed out loud. 'A hundred, where did they get that from? I've had about 50 I think. You can't believe anything they say mother.'

She smiled proudly. 'Well they do go on to say we went to London to receive your medals from the King as there's a picture of that too.'

His father was becoming impatient.

'What about the aeroplane, what's happening about that Lad? The Austin Ball.' He liked the name; it had a good ring to it.

'I went to see the Director of Air operations, Sefton Branker, in London last week. They've agreed to build two prototypes. Only the Austin Ball wasn't mentioned. They're calling it the Austin.'

157

'Don't be daft lad; I shall have a word with Herbert for you. The Austin Ball it will be. I shall make sure of it.' It was Albert Senior who initially suggested Austin as the builder of the plane. He was a director there and knew Herbert Austin personally. Father had given Albert shares in the company just a month before. Albert had been keen for them to work on producing a scout that would be as fast as the Fokkers and have the manoeuvrability of the Nieuport. The company had worked from his sketches and outline specifications.

'What happened at the war Office Albert?' Albert Senior had thought the summons from them was a promotion.

'They offered me promotion to Major. I turned them down flat. I am too young for a desk job and Commanding Officers are forbidden to fly within five miles of the enemy lines. That's not for me.'

His father looked distressed.

'You turned them down? You could have been a Major and you turned them down flat?' He was incredulous now. The boy was annoyed.

'You'd like the commander-in-chief's job of course, but I feel that a man should be older than I, for administrative work. I'm not a soldier and promotion doesn't interest me. It's fighting that I'm useful at. It's just a job and a duty.' Albert Senior was silenced by this.

They began getting ready for the ceremony late in the afternoon. His parents had new clothes for the occasion; Albert's uniform was smart and his medals shone. The Press took pictures of them leaving the house and entering the Nottingham Exchange Hall. He had dreaded the thing, but with Father's help, he had a speech ready. The hall was full when they went in. There were row upon row of grey suited professional middle aged men. The great and the good of the city were there; aldermen, councillors, factory owners and leaders of commerce. Albert senior as one of them sat in front of Albert, Mayor Pendleton in his robes, the town clerk in his white wig and Harriet in her new black and yellow hat.

The Mayor stood and the men were silent. He began by saying that:

'The Nottingham city Council have decided that Flight Commander Albert Ball, D.S.O. M.C., being a person of distinction within the meaning of the honorary freedom of the Boroughs Act 1885, he be admitted an honorary freeman of the City of Nottingham, in recognition of the great services rendered by him as an officer of the Royal Flying Corps in connection with the Operations of the British Expeditionary Force in France, and as a mark of the appreciations of his fellow-citizens of his bravery in the face of the enemy. Lieutenant Ball is without doubt, the greatest living expert in aerial warfare...'

Albert's face grew redder and redder. He looked down at the floor. He unfolded and refolded his speech as the Mayor rose to new heights of praise for him, with each new height; Albert squirmed lower in his chair. In front of him was a silver cask, a little bright box with a golden carving of his Nieuport on the top. This was where his certificate would be placed. When the mayor had finished speaking the aldermen and councillors applauded and he rose. His shaking hands betrayed his nerves as he began:

'It is indeed kind of the mayor to say such jolly decent things about me.' His voice faltered, the Town Clerk leaned forward and whispered:

'Take your time, my lad.'

'I think I shall have to,' Albert nervously whispered back. He cleared his throat.

'I do hope shall be a worthy successor to the honoured citizens whose names are already on the roll of the freemen. I am hoping to be out at the front again very soon. My only desire is to serve my country and my native city, of which I am justly proud.' It was as much as he could manage to say.

He sat down quickly and they applauded him again and again his face coloured and he squirmed like a pike caught on a hook.

Sunday April 8th 1917 Izel le Hameau aerodrome near Arras, France

Boom Trenchard coughed a loud rattling death knell of a cough. His head and throat felt heavy with the bronchitis. He should really have stayed in his comfortable bed at the Chateau but he felt more wretched sending Baring out to do his work than he did doing it himself. He had sent out Baring to do just that the day before but the news had been so grave he had become utterly determined to visit every squadron involved in tomorrow's big push personally.

Boom looked ill. His face was white and pallid and although he usually looked like a young man, today, despite his black hair, the signs of the stress were clearly lined in his face. The bronchitis had come hard on the heels of a nasty bout of German measles. He had heard all the jokes about that one. The General catching German measles had entertained the Messes for weeks. Now, there were big black circles underneath his eyes despite the relative comfort of his life at HQ. He had been saying for a long time that in order to maintain air superiority, the RFC needed faster, better planes. Output at home was not keeping apace with the speed of technology; as a result, German pilots were flying quicker, more agile machines. He had predicted losses in this battle and he had been sadly proven all too right. His force had lost 75

160

aircraft since April 3rd. How could he find sufficient replacement men and machines if they continued at that rate? The average age of the boys Trenchard led was 19. Their life expectancy at the front could be measured in hours.

From the start, his policy had been a simple one. The RFC would be used as an offensive force, flying over the German lines and engaging their machines. The one problem with the policy was that it meant that the allied pilots had to attack; the Germans could flee in relative safety. Now the appearance of faster slicker German machines and better trained pilots meant his force faced a deadly challenge. Some had argued that to slow the casualty rate he should take a more defensive stance but this he knew was nonsense. Any floundering on his part from the offensive would give the better equipped Germans Air superiority entirely. He would never allow that.

He had found so many nagging problems to deal with today. They had breakfasted early, on eggs as it was Easter Sunday. Trenchard had been infuriated by one letter he had received. They had flown off from André aux Bois, Trenchard in an RE8 and Baring in a BE2. Trenchard wanted to get a feel for the RE8 as it was one of the machines that there had been complaints about. It was disappointing in performance. Some of his squadron believed it to be a dud. That was a common occurrence for any relatively recently introduced plane at the Front. Pilots always wanted better machines.

They had spent time at the repair and stores section at St Omer. There were so many minor problems to attend to: machines with missing pieces, missing parts holding up repairs and men working on jobs that were taking forever. Then they had flown to Royal Naval Air Service, Number 3 squadron. They had told him the Vickers guns were jamming because they were using engine oil supplied by the admiralty. The

Navy pilots said it was inferior to the 32 squadron issue because the army stuff contained anti-freeze. Cold planes were devilishly hard to start. Mechanics had taken to filling the radiators with almost boiling water and several had been scalded as a result. Trenchard had ordered an analysis of both engine oils; that was Baring's suggestion.

Baring and Trenchard made quite a team. Baring was a writer and very popular amongst the men. He was an outstanding Aide because he was such a diplomat, a skill Trenchard made great use of. Baring had been a correspondent at several wars before this one. He could be Trenchard's eyes and ears at times. He provided Trenchard with a great barometer of the corps morale. Now, he was talking to the pilots in the hangars, encouraging them. Letting them know he shared their concerns about the speed of the RE8s that were to play such a vital role in tomorrow's attack.

Baring also shared a secret with the pilots that the General known to all as Boom, never knew of. Boom could be a gruff old thing at times. He had days when he was quite unkind to young pilots. Baring had evolved a system of punishments for Boom over which he was the sole judge and arbiter. If Boom was nasty to a young pilot, who suddenly thought he knew more than Boom about aerial warfare, then Baring might decide he was due for punishment number one. He would hide Boom's pipe for several hours. Boom was lost without his pipe; its loss frequently upset him quite deeply. Afterwards Baring would return the pipe and inform the young pilot that the punishment had been carried out. As yet, he had never got to punishment number 5. This was to be breaking the window of Boom's staff car so he had to be driven in a draught which he could not abide.

Boom sat now on his shooting stick, looking over the RE8 which had caused problems with the C.O. of number 100 squadron. An SE5 floated down from the direction his own plane had come some minutes earlier and taxied across to where his own plane stood. He had been speaking to Blomfield at Vert Galant about 56th Squadron's perceived difficulties with the SE5 which had disturbed him. It was his great hope that this particular aircraft would have a dramatic impact on the skies above the battlefield. This one was from 56th and landed so smoothly, he wondered if Blomfield had exaggerated.

A young boy in scruffy looking pilot's gear had landed the plane so neatly then belied his skill by falling flat on his face as soon as he got out of the cockpit. He was clearly in a hurry and looked around anxiously before dusting himself down again, and then coming their way at a pace. From the black mop of hair, the lack of goggles, the mess of a uniform, Trenchard knew who it was immediately, and what he wanted.

The boy Ball was Boom's great hope. His skill in shooting down enemy machines was a legend in the RFC. Ball was an inspiration to the other pilots and that was why Boom had allowed him back to the Front. Desperate times needed some inspiration. He was fearless; he had the heart of a lion and infinite courage it seemed. Boom had met him several times before. Their meetings at first were not entirely successful. Before he had established himself as a flyer, Ball had once come to see Boom. He had said he was fagged and in need of a rest. Boom had become quite used to these young lads who were puffed full of their own importance, to him they were extremely important. Most pilots were too afraid of him to come right out with it and ask for leave. Boom sent him on to Observation duties for a while until his nerves were restored. Since then, Ball had been more respectful. He was the most difficult and temperamental flyer in the corps and the best at attacking, whatever the odds.

He rushed over to them now, remembered at the last minute to salute then shook the General's hand firmly:

'Good afternoon General Trenchard, I was so sorry to have missed you at Vert Galant.' Ball's face was flushed.

'Good Afternoon, Captain Ball. Major Blomfield said you were on a test flight. Not too near the lines I hope.' The teething problems with the new plane had led Trenchard to put out an order that on no account was any SE5 to be flown over the trenches. He wanted to save the new machines as his surprise weapon in the forthcoming attack, and he wanted to make sure it was entirely reliable first.

Ball was anxious to show his compliance:

'Oh no Sir, I am aware of the order, it's why I have come to see you.'

Ball waited whilst the General finished his work with the C.O. then he and Boom walked together round the aerodrome.

Boon tried to speak kindly to the Lad. 'So Captain, what is the problem?'

'It's the SE5 Sir. I want to get up and after the Huns again and now I'm in a plane that's not allowed over the lines. It's slow. We have worked every day on improving it since the first one arrived, but it still climbs too slowly and doesn't manoeuvre like the Nieuport.' Ball looked at Boom to see how this had registered; he had learnt to be careful around Generals, especially this one.

Boom sighed and the sigh turned into a hoarse cough which he covered with his handkerchief. This young lad had fought like a one-man squadron the summer before. He knew the risks better than anyone and here he was again, anxious to be up and fighting just as soon as he had landed on French soil. Boom lowered his voice.

'Things have changed since last summer Ball. The Hun squadrons get bigger and bigger and they are faster than we are too. The time of the lone flyer is coming to an end; it's formations that matter now. All new planes take a while to show their true worth, there isn't a plane in the corps that someone has not complained about. Give the SE5 time and it will show its true colours.'

Ball looked at him directly again. He glanced at the wretched looking RE8s they were now passing and Ball became very aware, that the man he was talking to had the power to transfer him, to a squadron where he had to fly the dull witted things. He chose his words carefully and spoke slowly.

'While we are waiting Sir, I wondered if I couldn't have a Nieuport Sir, to take up and get at them again.'

Ball's directness made the General laugh; a rare event that awful month. He decided to be equally direct in his reply:

'And I was not impressed when your Father wrote to me making that same request just this morning Captain. Perhaps you will realise one day that I for one, do not respond to outside pressures. I am sure your father has better things to do than meddle in the affairs of the Corps.' Ball looked pained and said nothing. Boom decided not to pursue the point.

'However, I realise that your intentions are just due to your desire to do your job well. I'll see what planes we have available. Come and have dinner at HQ next week. We'll talk about this then. Three more squadrons to see, I must go, where the devil has Baring got to?' He saluted the boy who was smiling now.

'I have told Major Blomfield you are to be allowed all the time in the air that you want. As far as I am concerned Captain you have a roving commission, but the needs of your Squadron must always come first. Cheer O Captain Ball.'

The scruffy youngster saluted back, happily.

'Cheer O Sir. Oh and er Happy Easter Sir'

'Happy Easter Captain,' Boom marched away.

16.

Saturday May 5th 1917 The skies above Lens, France

He felt so old. Sometimes he blamed the fire. There was a time when just doing this; flying alone in a crystal sky, listening to the wail of his SE5 and the wind rushing through the tight wires in his wings, perching high in the vivid air behind the German lines, there was a time when this had been enough to blow all the cobwebs out of his mind and make him feel forever young again. Now he felt old.

Today had been a rest day and he'd been in the garden, but the pilots had started gathering at lunchtime, they were anxious for a fight. Blomfield had let two flights go up in the late afternoon. Two planes had turned back with the inevitable engine problems and he'd let Lewis and two others head off into the clouds. Ball was looking for cleaner air and to be honest, he still preferred to fight alone. In some of the scraps he'd had recently, he'd been more worried about flying straight into another RFC man than the Hun.

The fire really hadn't helped his mood. He'd had a good day and the number of victories he had achieved stood at 40. It made him the highest scoring allied pilot, so they arranged a concert in the mess. He played 'Humoresque' on the fiddle and they'd cheered and sang 'For he's a Jolly good fellow.' The Squadron band had played; it was the best in the RFC, of that he was sure. Then his happiness had been shattered by the incessant clamour of the station fire bell.

They ran out into the night from the warmth of the Mess and there was smoke billowing from the huts; from his hut. The hut he and Maxwell had finally finished that day. They were running with buckets from the farmhouse, some were beating the flames with blankets. It had taken hours to get it all out and dampen it down. He was sure at first a bomb had been dropped by the Germans in the centre of the aerodrome but Knaggs admitted he'd left a candle burning in his hut. Ball had exploded with temper for moments then had laughed with the others. Rebuilding the hut had taken him days.

His sharp eyes spotted two dots in his mirror. They were coming into his peripheral vision from the right and above him. He could see they were single seat scouts, probably albartri. He pulled the stick back and began climbing up to them, hauling his way through the air. He could hear their engines now and then one was suddenly behind him and coming in. He saw the white high wings with their jagged black crosses and the pale brown front of the plane in his mirror and immediately kicked down on the rudder and threw his plane vertically up into a high steep turn. For a moment, the horizon left him and he rode his luck high through the empty blue. He pushed high through the apex and then down into the turn and brought the machine down right behind the German. He had performed the Immelmann turn, named after the Hun whose trademark it was. Immelmann was dead now but his manoeuvre was still being used by both sides.

Ball slid the Lewis down and began to fire steadily. He was using tracers and could see them tearing into the underbelly of the German. The plane flew steadily on and he clung just beneath it, twice he had time to change drums on his gun. Now the Hun tried to escape him banking sharply to the right but Albert went with him, never more than fifty feet from him and blazing now with both the Vickers and the Lewis until the German contorted and spun down to the waiting grave below.

Then in an instant and coming from nowhere the second albatross was flying straight at him. The planes were flying straight at each other and neither would turn away. Bullets were passing one another midair to rip into both machines. They were coming closer and closer together. The Hun would ram him. The German plane was riding up, growing huge in front of him. He saw the bullet that tore through his engine and then a rush of hot black oil engulfed him. He was completely blinded. The passing from crystal air to blindness could only mean one thing; he waited for the inevitable explosion, the falling from the sky in a mangled machine.

There was nothing; a moment of pureness. He wiped the hot sticky black oil from his eyelids. Forcing them open with trembling hands he could see sky again. He had put the plane into a climb instinctively as the oil hit him. He pushed forward now to glide her down. At three thousand feet he levelled her off; he could see both broken albartri lying on the ground below him. He must have hit the second one an instant before she would have smashed him apart. He was shaking and he still had to get his plane home. He could not see well, there was oil all over the cockpit, the windscreen and himself. Everything had been given a dose of oozing hot castor oil.

168

He wanted to pray but could not find words. He tried to sing, he remembered the first two lines of her song about the Garden but then it dissolved into tears. He sobbed out loud. That was the closest he had ever come to it and it frightened him. He felt wretched and old and dead already. He felt like a murderer. All the killing had wearied him and he felt that it was ultimately himself that was dying. He needed to calm himself, but there was such a struggle inside him now. The tears refused to stop. He began breathing deeply.

Crossing over the lines, he saw two albartri alongside him. He found this strangely calming. He knew he had little ammunition left to fight them and gently banked off first one way then the other to keep his path home straight. They followed him for a few minutes and that was good too, because it kept him occupied. He did not want to think too much about things. He'd been given a glimpse of what death might feel like, what it might be to meet that angel full on. That could give you the worst nerves, nerves so bad they flew you home to a desk job and he did not want that.

His Oil pressure gauge was showing he had no pressure and very little oil. The bus was liable to overheat and seize up at any second. He did not want to die today, he wanted to get home. He'd realised the SE5 was a machine that could take so much punishment. They'd been pulling bullets out of his aircraft for weeks and he was flying her back now with many more. Every day, he'd been riding his luck through the sky and the clouds had been increasing.

Once he'd brought a machine back from a scrap flying her using the tail elevators alone. They'd been incredulous that he'd done it. Now he nursed the dying aircraft for forty five minutes through a darkening sky. He'd shed a final tear to see Vert

Galant below him and touched the lucky black cat on the undercarriage as soon as he had floated her down from the sky.

He wiped the rest of the oil from his face with a rag as he walked to the squadron hut. Marson was shocked at the state of him and Ball couldn't speak for a time. Marson had sat waiting for Ball to dictate the report but he couldn't calm down. He'd stood, wild eyed and red in the face. He seemed to be repeating the same words: 'God is very good to me. God must have me in his keeping. I was certain he meant to ram me.'

Granpa Marson placed a cup of hot sweet tea in the boy's shaking oily hands.

Friday April 6th St Albans, Hertfordshire.

The moon hung low over the garden and the snow fell silently. As she stood so close to him the world spun beneath them and the night revolved around them. She looked into those deep black eyes and drank him all up into her. Then she rubbed her cheek across the lapel of his coat and felt the snow there. She reached up and touched his face:

'You fly back to me. You come safely back here to me.' She whispered.

He smiled; the right side of his mouth always rose higher than the other when he did that. 'I'll bring back a Victoria Cross for you to wear and the war will be over.' He said.

'Just come back.' She pleaded, she wanted to say more but Bill chose this point to throw the tiny snowball he had gathered at Albert and the two began playing like boys do. Rolling each other in the snow and laughing.

He'd eventually agreed to talk to their parents about the wedding when he came home. He'd wanted to do everything all at once. He had decided to lend his best coat to Bill, they flew off in the morning and his kit would follow later. He would ask his Mother to collect the coat for him and that way she could meet the family. Her mother knew already she was sure. Mother could be quite formidable at times and had made several sharp comments about the fact that since they had first met, Albert had phoned, written or met Flora almost every single day. It did not take a mother's intuition to see what was happening.

The squadron had spent their last night at a hotel in Radlett village. They had a dinner and farewell party together. It was a subdued affair. They had all already packed off their kit and sent it on to France. Lewis and Rhys Davis had met two pretty girls in the village and invited them to join them but it was a very sober evening. Blomfield had already declared his intention that the 56th would be the first ever squadron to fly to France without losing a single machine along the way. Most of the pilots were staying at the hotel before going to the aerodrome first thing in the morning. Albert and Flora had eaten and then slipped away.

Her mother came out now into the garden and smiled at the two fighting boys. She stood next to Flora and they exchanged glances. Mother spoke kindly to her:
'Don't get cold Flora.'
'It has stopped snowing now mother, it was just a flurry really.'
'The garden still looks pretty, like a Christmas card I think. Will you sing for him tonight dear?'
Flora was sure: 'Yes, I'd like that very much. Albert wondered if he might phone his father first.'

171

'Yes of course.' Her mother smiled.

The maid brought them tea in the parlour. Albert had finally put all his business dealings with his father to one side. He and Bill had removed their slushy shoes and sat with her Father on the long sofa. The room was warm and light, they had lit a fire to frighten away the snow. Her mother kept cats and two of them lingered there with them to hear her sing. She was wearing a dress of purple crushed velvet with a full string of pearls round her neck. She had saved the special dress for his final performance. He made her sing again and again, the same song. He tried to be a camera; to capture her then and keep her. He tried to frame her in his memory; he was so aware that he was flying away. He tried to be a gramophone to record that lilting voice for playback later. The night was pulling breathlessly away from them.

Mother complained that her hands had grown tired from playing and Bill and her Father drifted away. The clock chimed nine and Albert rose. He stood close to her and said:

'Goodnight dear.' He kissed her cheek and she held it there with her finger as he turned and walked up the stairs. Her mother raised an eyebrow then smiled and announced she too was 'turning in.' Flora sat for a few moments alone in the firelight. The flames flickered and reflected across her eyes and she wondered. Then she heard his soft footfall on the stairs. She knew he would come to her.

He closed the door and put his finger to his lip to call down silence. He walked quickly to her and put both arms around her. He held her tightly in his arms and she felt covered by him completely. His mouth searched for hers and found it. Their lips caressed each other and stayed together, searching, imploring. Then she pulled away from him and rubbed her cheek against his. He looked down into her eyes:

172

'I love you, my dear.' He smiled. 'Cheer O'. Then he winked and was gone.

Later in the darkness, he found the poems she had given him. He found the one she had changed for him, crossing out the word you and replacing it with me. It read:

'For my absent loved one I implore Thy loving kindness. Keep him in life; keep him in growing honour...'

In another room below him she now tearfully prayed those very words.

He never saw her the next morning. It had been agreed she would stay away from the aerodrome. He could not bear goodbyes in public. He had the same arrangement with his mother. When he had left her the previous Saturday she had been in the cinema. He had kissed her and then left just before the film ended. He had liked that, leaving her all safe and warm in the dark. When the lights had come up again, the people in the cinema could not understand the funny woman, who had cried at a Charlie Chaplin film. Now he did the same to his lover, he had left her warm and safe in the dark.

Bill woke him and drove with him to the aerodrome. It was a fine and clear day. Flora's father drove them. There were thirteen dark brown SE5s lining up ready outside the sheds. They stood waiting the pilots that now fussed round them. They'd had one bit of bad news, Ball's friend Captain Foot, known to all as 'Feet' had crashed his car and would not be leading the squadron overseas that day. It was Lewis that now tied the Lead flyer's streamer to his plane. They had been issued with lifejackets for the flight across the channel. Some put them on, but no one took off wearing one. It seemed silly and they were confident of making the short hop across the channel all right. Blomfield was especially enjoying the morning. It had been some time since he'd been allowed to pilot his own plane. He was anxious for the boys to be about their business. He marched among them now with his little leather cane, looking like the ringmaster about to start the performance.

The aerodrome was quite busy that morning. There was a good turn out of people wishing the squadron a hearty 'Cheer O'. They were due off at 11 and by a quarter to, all the pilots were in their cockpits. Albert handed Bill a letter he had written to her that morning. He scribbled on the back now, 'God bless you dear.'

Blomfield gave the signal and Lewis led the planes out into the field. Albert saluted Bill, standing there in Albert's coat and taxied away, gathering speed as he moved with the other noisy birds across the field. His plane hurried forwards and leapt upwards and he was full of a sense of leaving for now and forever. It was a cloud that had hung above him for days. He took his place amongst the flying machines, as one by one they turned into the wind, stood tall and took off; droning out across the skies together, leaving behind them only silence and the lisping English wind.

17.

Monday May 7th 1917 Vert Galant aerodrome, near Douellen, France

Clouds. They had crept in from the east. Their build-up had been gradual. The first waves had been gentle rolling white mists and had come in streams. Then bigger, thicker more cavernous cloud mountains had followed those providing great screens of white in the air. Gradually, the grey ones, heavy with rain, had slowly made their way over from the reserves. Now there were thick banks of invisibility hanging in the sky, they carried such a threat of storms with them. They had invaded the blue and wrung the crystal brightness from the air. They had changed the landscape of the sky completely. Each seemed lined with the threat of death, of man and machine, falling in flames from the air. Now they lined up, rolling over one another, massing and swaying, ever-growing, crowding the sky. They had put the sun out and hidden all the horizons. Now their growing thickness promised rain and if they clashed great sheets or forks of flashing lightning and the dull rumble of thunder like the artillery bursting below would swathe the earth.

Blomfield marched steadily across the aerodrome, watching the sky. Things had turned decidedly murky. The air was thick with cumulus clouds that had floated over from the east. It was not enough to threaten operations, but it would make the patrol a more difficult one. Visibility meant everything to a pilot. He watched Ball checking over his plane. He thought of the letter he had received from Newall at Wing HQ that morning, asking for all Ball's recent combat reports since he returned to the Front. Douglas Haig, who ran the whole show, was meeting Ball in two days time. The letter must mean that Ball's exploits had attracted his attention. It had to be the recommendation for a Victoria Cross, Ball had surely earned it. They had awarded one to Leefe-Robinson last year for shooting down a Zeppelin over London. He'd been shot down on his first flight over the more dangerous skies of France; skies Ball had conquered and made his own. Blomfield knew exactly what aerial combat meant. He knew too well the risks he was asking these boys to take, every single day of their short and burning lives. He read the reports and he wrote to the parents of the fallen and pilots had the furthest to fall. Simple science told you that pilots fell fastest of all.

He saluted Ball and raised his cane with a twitch. The meeting with Pretyman at Savy had gone as he had expected. Wing had communicated their concerns about the Circus; the growing red threat. It had started with one quick albatross flyer that had cut Corps aircraft out of the sky accurately and from a distance. His plane was painted bright red. They nicknamed him Le Petit Rouge. Rumours and stories about him grew and grew. Then it seemed there was more than one red plane. There were great formations of them, swooping down from the sun and killing allied airmen. Plundering them from the sky like great red crows; the red baron and his travelling circus, that was the story, the rumour, the new legend. The truth was large formations of a new type of Albatross scout which seemed quicker and more manoeuvrable than anything the allies had. The skies were suddenly filling with thin red planes, flown by experienced fighters who were keen for a quick kill and almost always got it. They were led by Manfred Von Richtoffen.

Two days before, Blomfield and Marson had met with some gunners from the anti-artillery batteries. They had described to him exactly where the planes of the Richtoffen Jasta were fond of congregating every evening. He'd asked permission from wing to send up his fullest force against them. It had been agreed. The darkening skies and showers that were falling had led everyone to believe that this would end as a 'dud' day but the phone had rung whilst Blomfield had been at tea. Operations were to proceed that day as planned.

Orders had come in from Wing two days before, there was to be a regular morning and evening patrol of the corps best and newest fighters over the German airfields between Cambrai and Douai to try to force the enemy into action. The Spads from 19th Squadron were to meet with the Sopwith Triplanes of RNAS 8th Squadron and the long line of SE5s that Blomfield now checked and counted. This was a familiar ritual to him. He liked to count out every patrol and then count them in again.

The size and speed of the new Hun squadrons meant Blomfield had decided to make a bold statement; he was sending them all up. There were eleven planes in the line. If this really was the circus they were going up against, they'd need all three flights to fight up there and all the experience and luck they could gather. The boys were confident, they had been scoring well in recent days, Blomfield knew that this might be a real test for them. They were building up combat experience and experienced fighters live longer but the new type Hun machine was quicker then them and flown by pilots who knew all the tricks.

The boys jumped down from their machines or crawled out from beneath them. They stood around him in their flights and he gave them their orders. Ball was flight commander; they'd need his tenaciousness today. He would lead Maxwell and Knaggs in A flight. Crowe would lead Leach, Rhys Davis and Chaworth-Musters in B flight whilst the South African, 'Duke' Mientjes would lead Hoidge, Lewis and Melville in B flight. That was just about full squadron strength at that moment. They would set off at seventeen thirty hours and fly over the lines south of the Bapaume to Cambrai Road, then patrol North east between Cambrai and Douai. Their patrol area would be overlapped by the Spad S7s and they were also to look out for the support from the Sopwith triplanes from the Royal Naval Air Service. His eyes narrowed as he looked from face to face:

'You should expect to meet up with HA sooner rather than later. The Richtoffen circus has been seen in that area. You'll need to keep your wits about you today Gentlemen as I expect you to be busy. There are banks of cumulus cloud running anywhere from two thousand to ten thousand feet, so adjust your positions accordingly. 'A' flight will fly at seven thousand feet, 'B' flight at nine and 'C' at ten.

177

Keep a sharp eye out for HA and before you attack anything, make sure it's not one of ours. Keep an eye out for one another at all times. If you become separated at any point then fly to the rendezvous point ten thousand feet above Arras. Keep an eye on your fuel, make sure you leave enough to get home and if you run out of ammunition or your gun jams, come straight home. Remember that the Vickers will work better if you warm it up with short bursts first. I wish you the best of luck gentlemen.'

He saluted them and his boys dashed off. They checked everything again and one by one the engines woke and began their wailing roar. He and Marson walked along the line. Saluting each man as he taxied away across the aerodrome, Ball responded with a smile and a wave as he led them away. The planes formed into one group of three and two groups of four. They rushed across the field, leapt into the air and began making their steady climbs up into the clouds.

Blomfield began making his way back across the empty field. The mechanics walked back through the rain which was falling steadily now to the hangars and the long wait. He walked slowly so Marson could walk alongside him. The two men said little as they drank tea together in Marson's hut, one ear on the aerodrome outside and one anxiously awaiting the phone's shrill ring. They were used to this long wait together. Blomfield's second cup was barely cold when they heard a stuttering engine making its way back to the field. They saw it come down, wearily and bouncing slightly. It was Melville; his machine was smoking and running horribly rich. He'd stayed with the rest for as long as he could but could tell from the sound his machine wasn't fit to fly that day.

An hour passed and the rain came in waves. The aerodrome grew darker as day began to withdraw. At twenty past seven, Maxwell flew in low and landed his plane smoothly. He had crossed the lines with the rest just south of Bapaume but they had run into a heavy cloud bank over Bourlon Wood. They'd soon separated from B and C flights and he could see them no more. As his flight flew on, the cloud grew thicker and thicker. Soon he could see no other plane in the sky. Ball and Knaggs had gone. He flew on through the valleys of the clouds for a while but his fuel was low and he decided to turn home. He missed the fall of Roger, Roger Musters.

Roger Chaworth-Musters had been flying high up, to the right of 'C' flight when he had seen the German plane. Only Rhys Davis had seen him bank off and fall away in a wide curve to chase the tail he had glimpsed through the clouds. He had decided to go for the machine with his Vickers and dropped down behind her and prepared to rake her. He fired a short burst from the Vickers to warm the gun and the Hun pushed down on the rudder and shot upwards. Musters was too slow to react, he didn't pull away with her and soon she came down again right behind him. He tried to bank to the right to avoid her, but from the cockpit of his Albatross, Werner Voss, the most accomplished flyer in Jasta Boelke, gleefully squeezed the trigger, spurting burning lead into the petrol tank of Musters' plane which exploded. The flames tore the machine from the sky, and it fell in burning pieces. The first of the fallen that day was Roger, Roger Musters.

Monday May 7th Hackett's Farm.

When the tree had fallen, it had happened in slow motion for her. She had noticed the cow, which should not have been anywhere near the wood and it distracted her. She had turned to ask the girls how it had got there, but then Amy had kicked the tree, and it had crashed down. By the time she had called out, it was too late. The animal

179

screamed when the falling branches of the tree had knocked it to the ground. They all ran to it then. It was down on its front legs which were twisted back under it. It was crying out deeply and pitifully.

Violet climbed over to the other side of the fallen trunk and she and Flora began trying all they could, to pull the thing off the stricken animal, but it would not budge either way, it was too heavy. Amy was despatched and ran down to the farmhouse. The cow would not stop crying. Flora tried to reach through the branches to calm her but the branches were thick and heavy. She began snapping off twigs and brushing them aside, trying to get to it. Hackett appeared with Amy and a thick rope. He passed one end to Violet and she wound it round the oak trunk. Then she climbed back to them and they all joined in the strain.

Hackett and his tug of war team, Violet, Flora, Beatrice and Amy pulled hard on the rope. Flora's boot's dug into the damp earth of the woods as she pulled, her hands gripping the rope tightly. They began with steady pressure but that didn't move it. So Hackett moved to the front and began sharp tugs which he counted off to them. The girls groaned and panted. The fourth sharp tug moved the tree right off the cow. They released the rope and went over to it. Hackett spoke quietly to it:

'Now then girl, how did you get up here?' The cow remained kneeling, her legs were broken. Hackett knew. He turned to the girls.

'Her legs could be broken. I'll phone the Vet.'

Violet lit a cigarette and smoked it pensively. Beatrice followed Hackett back to the farmhouse through the gloom with the rope and Amy and Flora stroked and tried to comfort the quiet cow.

'She must have got out of the field where the hedges are thin.' Flora stroked the thick black neck. The cow seemed to be crying.

'I told Hackett we needed to repair those.' She hated to see something suffering like this.

Violet blew out a long wreath of smoke into the darkening wood. She had no time for sentimental thoughts. It was just another animal, just a big piece of meat.

'If its legs are broken the vet will shoot it. I haven't had a nice sirloin steak for years...' Flora threw Violet her most evil glance.

'Violet, don't say that!' Her voice was betrayed by a nervous giggle.

Inside the farmhouse Hackett stood alone in his front room. In his hand, he held an envelope with a telegram inside. The room was spinning round him as he looked at it. He had seen the scout's bicycle come down the farm drive as he telephoned the vets. How could a small boy dressed in green on a bicycle fill him with such utter dread and fear? It was the same boy that brought him a telegram some months before and then Tony was dead. The same boy that had brought him news of Jack's ship going down; they used the boy to bring bad news. He looked down at the envelope. What if he didn't open it, what if he threw it into the fire there and then? No, he had to know which one had been taken from him this time. He tore it open.

The cow rolled over. It had attempted to stand but its legs had buckled back under it. It was clearly in pain. Flora stoked its brow and Amy cooed to it, talked to it as if it was a little girl. Violet was cutting branches off the trunk with the axe and shifting them, clearing a way round the cow. Beatrice rejoined them. She brought a saw with her from the barn and she and Flora began cutting through the great trunk again. The rain was dripping down through the branches of the trees above them as they worked.

181

A single magpie cackled its way through the wood. Slowly Hackett made his way back to them. Flora noticed how drawn he looked. He stood with his hands on his hips disconsolately.

'There's no one in at the vets so I sent for the slaughter man. The beast is in pain, its legs are broken and it's for the best.' Flora looked at the poor animal suffering before her.

'Are you all right Mr Hackett? You don't look well.' He looked up at her from the distance.

'I've had some news; my boy Jedd. He's been wounded but he's all right. He's coming home next week. He reckons he'll be able to work with me in a month and he won't have to go back. Shrapnel it was, in the thigh.' Hackett sounded lost, good news was something he had never expected again.

'Oh that is wonderful news Mr Hackett; you shall have some proper help again.' Flora smiled. Hackett looked at her fondly.

'I've got proper help now girl.'

They made the cow as comfortable as they could and the slaughter man arrived half an hour later. Except this being the upside down world it was since the war started, the slaughter man was in fact a woman. She was a big armed, white haired, battle axe of a farmer's wife wearing a wide, blood stained apron. She marched into the wood and looked at the cow, then took a revolver from the pocket of her apron. She pointed it at the forehead of the cow and Flora put her fingers in her ears. A single shot burst out and echoed back through the trees. The cow spurted an arc of blood then fell still, a great lifeless lump. Beatrice retrieved the rope and the girls puffed and strained, dragging the heavy carcass back down to the farmyard on a trailer. The light thickened and the sun burst briefly on them through the clouds and then gradually the blackness descended, covering the farm and the rain drenched fields.

18.

Monday May 7th Clouds above France

It was over the Douai-Cambrai road that Lothar saw the first of the new type of British plane. He was leading the Richtofen Jagdstaffel on their usual evening patrol. The Jagdstaffel or Hunting section, had been renamed Richtofen just days before to celebrate the achievements of his brother, Manfred. Manfred had reached a total of 52 aerial victories and had become the ace of aces. Right now, he was hunting in the forests of Silesia, preparing to meet the Kaiser. He had handed control of his Jagdstaffel to his brother with a simple handshake a week before.

Lothar had grown accustomed to living in his brother's giant shadow. In the rush to the war in 1914 they had both joined Cavalry regiments. Manfred had fought on the Eastern Front and Lothar had ridden through Belgium but both had soon realised that cavalry would have a very limited role to play in this largely static war. It was Manfred who had taken to the skies first and encouraged Lothar to follow him. At this time, Lothar was training troops in Luben and was certainly ready for some sort of new challenge. Manfred had flown him home and Lothar's first taste of his brother's celebrity status had come as the people of the village gathered round to see the Richtofen brother's plane.

Manfred had pulled strings to get Lothar posted into his own Jagdstaffel. Lothar had been sent home from Pilot training school after exhausting himself in February. Then at the beginning of March he had joined the famous Jasta 11, his brother's squadron.

The German government, unlike the British, had soon seen the propaganda value of its most successful pilots. As Manfred's toll of victories grew, he was feted by the powers that be. His image appeared on postcards for the people back in Germany to collect. His great mentor was Von Boelke, and he was heartbroken the day Boelke was killed in a collision. Manfred had given Lothar a pair of his old flying gloves which had become a lucky talisman for Lothar. He wore them now as he led his Keffe on patrol. The government saw the value of two noble Prussian brothers leading a Jagdstaffel; in truth, this had allowed Lothar the chance to jump the normal pecking order in the Jasta.

The spirits among the Jasta were high, they were gaining victories every day and most were now experienced fighters. They were flying out of a new airfield at Roucourt and were billeted in the castle there, which was comfortable and made a grand setting for the work they did. Lothar had now a total of 18 victories in combat; a long way behind Manfred but he was on his way to being awarded the Blue Max medal. The difference between the fighting styles of the brothers had been pointed out by Manfred. He claimed that he was a hunter, and it was on the hunting grounds, shooting wild boar from horseback that he had become such a deadly marksman. Lothar, he had said was not a hunter, but a shooter.

Lothar did not mind this, if he lacked Manfred's determined poise, he made up for it with energy and a fierce determination to gain as many victories as he could for himself. There were days when he wanted to be seen in his own right as a flyer, not just someone else's brother and now Manfred was at home, he had the perfect opportunity for this. He signalled to Wolff, who was flying as his wingman to prepare for an attack on the British planes. Wolff had inherited the Jasta's need for talismans. He flew in a ridiculous lucky nightcap which was the butt of many jokes in the Jasta. Besides him flew Wilhelm Allmenröder, Eberhardt Mohnicke and Georg Simon; all experienced fighters with growing reputations.

They had been amused by a report in the German press the day before. The English, growing ever more fearful of Manfred had put together a squadron of crack pilots. Their role in the war was to shoot down Manfred, just that. They had cameras in their planes to record the event for a film. The successful pilot that killed Manfred would be given his own plane, promotion, a Victoria Cross and five thousand pounds. Lothar had long ago learned not to believe the newspapers but the report had shown the English recognised Manfred's importance.

They had broken through thick cloud and there were four English planes approaching them. Lothar saw that they were the newest type of English scout. Suddenly the skies were full of diving and falling aircraft. One dived down on Lothar, its machine guns spurting lead into Lothar's tail. He hit down hard on the rudder and took the lighter, faster albatross into a sharp loop. He came back behind the British machine and raked fire into it before the pilot pulled steeply away.

Simon was also right in the thick of it now. A British scout had attacked him but he had managed to curve back round behind it and now was intent on destroying his enemy. He fired his Maxim gun hard into it but the pilot jerked his machine into a vertical bank and then a fast corkscrew spin that Simon could not follow. The plane came out below him and the allied pilot immediately attacked another of the Jasta, pouring lead from his Vickers gun from just fifty yards away. He tore the machine to pieces and Leutenant Wolfgang Von Pluschow fell away to crash down to the ground.

The skies were thick with planes diving and bursting with rattling machine guns. Planes swooped in and out of the clouds. Lothar and Allmenröder flew together, climbing higher, searching the skies continually for allied aircraft. They came across a British scout at 12000 feet and engaged him at once from beneath, firing into his fuel tanks. He dived away from them sharply and then they were the prey. A second machine flew in from behind and above them with busting machine guns. Again, Lothar dived down deeply and evaded his pursuer by banking up into thick clouds. Then the air was suddenly clear and Lothar found himself high up in the empty sky, above the thickest clouds, alone. The evening was drawing in and the drizzle had turned to rain. He felt cold and damp in the cockpit of his albatross D III. A thin red fighter plane they called the Haifisch or shark. The shark was a match for any British machine, Lothar was sure. It could out-climb their fighters and was faster than they were.

He flew on alone for almost an hour. He could not know it, but how busy his fellow fighters were at the time. 56th Squadron were split up and flew now alone or in pairs around their patrol area. After shooting down Von Pluschow, 'Duke' Meintjes dived on a lone red albatross, just east of Lens. His adversary spotted him and climbed away, the two circled each other for a time, both men trying to get on the other's tail. It was the German machine that finally gained the advantage; it pulled into a tight reverse and shot accurately into Mientjes cockpit. A bullet tore through Mientje's right wrist. In the tearing pain of it, Mientjes let go of the stick and his plane plummeted. Mientjes was fighting unconsciousness as his plane fell, the ground roaring up to meet him. He used his left hand to grab the joystick and land the machine. As it stopped, he fainted but was soon pulled from the plane by British infantry and taken to a Field hospital.

Rhys Davis found himself under an attack from a red albatross. In almost his first taste of aerial fighting he was soon in trouble, coming under fire of a far more experienced opponent. He could not shake the thing from his tail and his opponent was diving and climbing behind him, showering his machine with lead. There were bullet holes in the tail of Rhys Davis' plane but it was the ones in the engine that were most worrying. He could see it was leaking water and the engine was faltering. Then the albatross broke off the chase. It was Wolff and his gun had jammed. Rhys Davis glided the stricken plane down, he hoped to reach Bellevue aerodrome but two miles west of Arras he was forced to put her down in a field, the engine had died completely. He knew just how close he'd come to dying that day.

'B' flight had already lost both Musters and Rhys Davis when John Leach and Cyril Crowe downed an albatross east of Vitry. The two were separated and Leach flew on alone. Suddenly an albatross, hitherto veiled by white cloud, fired fiercely into the side of his cockpit. The bullet went straight through his leg, severing it. The plane fell and he fought through waves of deadly faintness to bring it down. Still only half-conscious he managed to pull the bird level before it hit the earth. He was dragged from the cockpit and taken to a field hospital where Canadian surgeons urgently tried to save the useless bleeding leg.

Crowe had flown on alone when a red kite shot from the clouds. It came straight for him firing continually. One bullet flew so close to him it cut through the string of his goggles and they flew from his face into the sky. The two planes missed each other by inches and Crowe flew nervously on. He was attacked again by a formation this time, but managed to evade them. It was above Fresnoy that he finally found Ball.

The two flew together for a time with Ball as the leader. The rain was coming down thickly now and both were cold and wet. They had been up for almost three hours and fuel was running low. Both knew they would not make it back to Vert Galant that night but would need to seek shelter in a closer aerodrome. Ball had been in several fights and his guns had jammed more than once. He had banged his wrist on the Lewis badly in one attack and it ached, he thought it might be broken. His head ached and his vision was becoming increasingly blurred. He was still shaking from the previous fight which for him was unusual. He was tired; he had been concentrating so hard for one hundred and eighty minutes. Each minute might require a thousand snap decisions; decisions on which his life depended. He felt old and tired and in pain. He needed a bath and a rest. He needed a good meal and a cup of tea. He needed to go home. He was sick of all the killing. Sick to death of it.

Then Lothar flew below him. Ball saw the shark slither through the clouds. He shot two crimson falling very lights into the sky as a signal to Crowe and dived.

Lothar found his sky suddenly full of English planes. He expected most of his Jasta had flown home by now, but he had hung on; he expected to go home with a victory that day. He did not want to disappoint Manfred, who wanted him to get to twenty aerial victories whilst Manfred was away. Now a plane was diving on Lothar, its machine guns rattling. The first sign had been holes appearing in the fuselage around him as the white tracer bullets ripped into the fabric. He banked to the left as a second plane poured holes into his wings. The second attacker overshot but the first was coming back, on Lothar's tail so he glided the shark menacingly round. As he did so, a third attacker fired on Lothar's plane but this too overshot and climbed away.

For a while they mirrored one another in the air from a distance. Both men knew their planes so well they were able to imitate each and every movement. They banked together, climbed together, dived and then pulled away. Lothar had seen the red spinner. He was enjoying this so much but it required such intense passionate concentration. He danced in the air with Ball, the 'English Richtofen'. The two brothers flew together and then around one another. Then Lothar reacted quicker and pulled round Ball. Lothar came at him head on, the bullets sliced the air and Lothar climbed into the clouds above him.

In and out of the thick clouds they twisted. Barely seeing each other, they exchanged burning metal again, roaring at one another. Despite his blurred vision, this time Ball's aim was perfection and Lothar smelt petrol. He knew the smell for him, could be deadly. Ball had hit his tank and Lothar dived down. His shark was bleeding and falling and he quickly crashed down in a field. He saw Ball's plane enter the thick pillar of cloud as he climbed from a broken cockpit into the mud.

Just for a second, just for a split fraction of a second, Albert finally relaxed. His head slumped back momentarily then drunkenly lilted forward. The wrist he had broken slipped from the stick and if there had been one last final horizon for him, it was suddenly, so faintly revolving.

And the veins of sunlight burst the cloud with spears of molten air. The spears strafed the plane wantonly, but for once, just for once; today's piercings were ineffectual; enfilading the fuselage with light.

Albert Ball awoke with a start; he had been dreaming about clouds again; endless grey mountains of cloud that were smothering all his horizons.

Her yellow dress had fluttered in his air and the moon had stayed still.

The black castor oil, the molten soot, the liquid ash was dripping as the plane was tipping. The butterfly's last flight was ending in a beautiful one hundred and eighty degree twirl, so slow, so subtle and so deadly said the oil with its drip, drip, drip.

When he opened his eyes for the penultimate time, he was flying and the clouds of his dreams were deep. His head felt so thick and heavy he could barely lift it. He barely had time to register the engine had died, and the mirror showed smoke trails behind him, when the cloud burst into air, and he saw he was low and flying upside down. He tried to wrench the joystick just once more but had no time; the machine began crashing through the tops of the trees. The earth welcomed him, redeeming him at last from the air. The plane snapped feebly. It broke his back, almost bit off his head and smashed his legs as it grinded him into the ground.

Monday May 7th 1917 Annoeullin, Near Lille, France

Cecille Deloffre loved Fashoda. Other locals had told her the old farmhouse was ruined because it was haunted. Every single occupant it had ever had had fled from the place in fear for their lives, they said. She didn't believe a word of it. Her father had told her before he went to the war; Fashoda was in ruins because its owners were bad farmers who had no respect for the land. That made sense to her.

Cecille was nineteen; an attractive dark haired girl with long brown hair and deep green eyes. She liked the peace of the evening. She worked the land with her mother all day and enjoyed the escape of each evening. The farmhouse was lived in by rats, so she avoided it and scouted the land around it.

She heard the stuttering engine first of all. It did not surprise her; there was a German aerodrome nearby. When the Germans first came to Annoeullin, her mother had been afraid. She'd said the soldiers would rape them and for three days she hid Cecille in a dark, dank cellar. Now the soldiers and airmen paid them for eggs and potatoes. Sometimes they whistled at her, but usually they left the two women alone.

Now she realised that the engine noise was growing louder and that the engine was dying. She saw from the cockades that it was a British plane, flying very low and upside down and bursting through the clouds. It went straight down into the earth and shattered. There was a crash as it fell to pieces.

She gathered her skirts around her and ran. When she saw him slumped there, she thought he was dead. She went to him, his fallen head in the wrecked plane. She wanted to help the poor broken boy so with she gently lifted him free from the wreckage. He was so small, it was not hard for her to lift his body from the shattered twisted mess of wood and metal and flimsy bits of broken butterfly wings. She had lifted heavier lambs than this.

She placed him down on the earth beside her and cradled his head in her arms. He was just breathing; she could hear him lying there in the growing darkness. She looked down at him. There was a bruise on his cheek but no other sign that he had been hurt. He was a good looking boy with thick black hair and a smooth white skin. His eyes opened and he looked at her. My, she was pretty, his angel of death. He almost smiled then his eyes closed again and he slumped forward. She bathed his forehead with a tear.

191

'Mon petit papillon, ah ma petit.'

He had gone. A single red poppy fluttered silently to the ground.

Leutnant Franz Hailer found the girl holding the dead pilot. He, his brother Carl and two friends had watched the crash through binoculars from their aerodrome. They had rushed to the scene; Hailer had spotted the red nosecone on the plane so they had known exactly who it was. Cecille let them lift his body from her then she waited with them until an ambulance arrived to take him to the field hospital. The Germans searched both the pilot and the plane thoroughly. She saw Hailer take a thin red book from the boy's pocket and a white handkerchief with the letter 'A' embroidered on the corner. They told her in rough French that he was Albert Ball, the 'Le Richtofen Anglais'.

She walked alone into the dark.

19.

Monday May 7th 1917 Vert Galant.

Blomfield could not face another cup of tea. He was struggling to hide the panic that was rising inside him with each passing minute. He had to keep a calm exterior at all times but he was deeply anxious and found it hard to hide. It was eight o clock. He'd counted out eleven planes at five thirty. They had enough fuel, at a real push, for three hours flying time. So far he'd counted back in just three planes.

Knaggs had returned five minutes ago. He'd been in some real scraps but had not managed a victory. He was dictating his combat report to Marson. It became clear as Blomfield heard his account that they'd run into the circus that day. He'd fought alongside Ball and had rescued Lewis from a tight spot. He'd also seen Arthur Rhys Davis down behind the English lines, apparently safe and well. That was four out of eleven Blomfield could count off, seven missing airmen. He left Marson to go

through the details of the report with Knaggs and went out into the night.

Along the edges of the hangars he could see the waiting ground crews. They leant

disconsolately against the hangar doors. Here and there he could see a glowing ember

of a cigarette through the dark. Time crawled when you waited. He could hear a

distant engine now, he became sure of it. The sound awoke the men. They called to

one another. In the sky, almost completely dark now he began to make out a shape,

then another. There were two returning SE5s, he could tell by their shape now.

Blomfield narrowed his eyes and searched for a streamer on a wing that would signify

one of his three missing flight commanders. He could not see one. It was not until

the planes had landed and taxied to the hangars that he saw it was Lewis and Hoidge.

Lewis spent a few minutes looking over the bullet holes in his tail fins before

bounding over to Blomfield. The two men looked across at the depleted line of

aircraft. Lewis spoke quietly and with a weighted voice:

'Where is the rest of the squadron?' Blomfield breathed calmly before he spoke.

'Rhys Davis was seen down safely. Melville had fuel problems and Maxwell got lost

in cloud cover. Knaggs came back five minutes before you did. Did you see anyone

come down?' Lewis looked into the sky. It became dark so quickly in France.

'It was the circus alright. We hit one group of four and one got right on my tail, until

Knaggs shot him off. I found Hoidge at the rendezvous. Fuel was looking decidedly

grim by then so we came home. We saw no one else other than Huns. No news of

Duke or Crowe? What about Ball, he'll get back, he always does.'

Blomfield bit his lower lip. 'I'll phone Bellevue, maybe some of them just had the

fuel to get there.'

193

Hours passed. Marson wrote reports and telephoned everyone and everywhere he could think of for news. There was a mood of despair hanging low over the aerodrome. In the mess the men were quiet and absorbed. Hoidge had claimed one victory on his report but there were no celebrations for that. All the bright young hope of this morning was lost somewhere in the clouds.

The first good news came from Naval 8th Squadron. Cyril Crowe had landed safely there with just a drop of fuel left in his tank. Then Blomfield could count off his fellow Scot, John Leach. He was particularly fond of Leach, a big honest sort of flyer. He was in a Canadian Field Hospital with critical wounds to the leg.

Long after midnight, Blomfield still felt heavy with a sense of loss. There was no word of Mientjes, Musters or Ball. Tired air crews finally gave up waiting and went to bed. Marson finally ran out of people to phone.

The following day the clouds still hung over them. Crowe came home and told them he'd last seen Ball flying into a cloud bank in pursuit of a red albatross. Mientjes was found wounded in a military hospital. Many still clung to belief in their champion; Ball was a Prisoner of War somewhere or hiding out behind the enemy lines. Blomfield told Trenchard Ball was missing and both men wrote to Ball's father and Musters' parents as well. It was a part of the job that Blomfield hated, but he tried to relay to both sets of parents there was still some hope, either man might have been taken prisoner. Lewis flew Ball's Nieuport back to the aircraft depot. Ball would not be coming back. Blomfield felt morale drop steeply as the day dragged on. He ordered a Mess concert that evening and the squadron turned out together.

You could cut the air with a knife as Lewis stood to sing in the draughty French barn, lit by candlelight. He sang 'Requiem' and all the men knew who it was for:

'Under the wide and starry sky,

Dig the grave and let me lie.

Glad did I live and gladly die,

And I laid me down with a will.

The squadron stood as one to applaud him and remember the boy they had almost known well and now would never return.

The next day, the Germans buried Captain Albert Ball with full military honours in the burial place of their own. Plot 99 of the German military cemetery at Annouellin became his final resting place; surrounded by sixteen hundred and ninety two German soldiers and pilots. He was given flowers, a wooden coffin and some allied Prisoners of War were asked to attend. There were many German Officers there, all in full military dress. Cecille went along and stood in the shadows. Later she placed a posy of her own, the first of many, on the grave of her petit papillon.

Sunday June 10th 1917 Sedgeley House, The Park, Nottingham.

'Why Miss Young, Thanks so much for coming. It's good to see you again.' Albert Senior shook Flora's hand. He was suited in black and with a black tie. He introduced Flora to Cyril who was in his RFC uniform and ushered her in to the front room. Lol had picked her up from the station and would drive her to the church.

The maid brought tea and they sipped quietly. The clock on the mantelpiece ticked loudly. Outside it was a fine and clear day. Arthur stood with his back to the empty grate:

'Harriet's taken it all very badly I'm afraid. It's been a terrible time for all of us but it was the waiting for news that upset her. She's not at all well and won't be down today I'm afraid, Miss Young.'

Flora understood. When the news had finally come through, when they had finally known what happened and that he was dead; her life had drained out of her. There had been three long dark weeks between the official announcement he was missing and the German announcement of his death. There had been questions in the House of Commons about his fate and there had been the announcement that he was alive and a Prisoner of War. It was the times when hopes were raised that had been the hardest to bear. She had lived by the telephone. Then there had been Albert Senior's broken voice on the telephone:

'He's gone love, his plane crashed. The Germans have sent a message saying that they buried him.'

She'd known it so long but she still felt the wind leave the pit of her stomach. The sobs had overcome her and her mother finished the conversation. She had held the little golden bracelet he had given her in her hands and flooded it with her tears.

Someone had taken away her future, had stolen away her first love. She knew she could never replace that. There was coffin for them to mourn, no funeral, just an absence and for her some days it felt like the absence of air. His letters had continued arriving at her house, even after he was officially missing. The one she had sent him which begged him to come back to her safely was returned unopened. She had burnt it without reading it again.

For days she had lived in darkness and not come out of her room. Some days she blamed him, he could have come home. Other days she blamed herself for not begging him sooner. She had no appetite for working on the farm.

They announced that he had been awarded the Victoria Cross. It was gazetted two days ago. The Victoria Cross, the VC, what he had wanted. On the days she felt most wretched; it was as if he had given his life for a silly piece of bronze.

She knew a time was approaching when he would have been dead longer than she'd known him whilst he was alive. They had thirteen days together; he had been dead for thirty two. They'd written for five weeks, now he had been dead for four. There had even been a morning she had woken believing him to have been just a dream. Now his father was real and big in front of her.

'You must call me Flora, Mr Ball,' she said.

'Only if you will call me Albert, Flora. My son made no secret of how fond of you he was of you.' His voice faltered and he took a handkerchief from his waistcoat pocket and blew his nose.

Flora had met Albert Senior before. Albert had sent his parents to St Albans to retrieve the coat he leant to Bill. He had planned it that way; he wanted them to meet before the engagement became official. He manipulated the two great loves of his life together. Flora had found Harriet especially charming when they came to St Albans. You could tell how much she worried about both her boys. It must be agony for her now.

'So Mrs Ball won't be coming to the service, I am sorry to hear that.' Albert frowned, he looked paler than the last time she had seen him, older too.

'No, she hasn't the heart for it today. She's not been getting up at all most days I'm afraid. That boy meant the world to her really.'

Lol bustled in, looking shiny in black but so tired. Her eyes were pink and lined. 'We'd better be going to the church now, Flora.' His sister and his lover were like two pretty blackbirds as they climbed into the car.

The people of Nottingham turned out for Albert in full. Ten thousand of them lined the solemn streets to see the procession. The police band led them out from the Exchange Hall. The Mayor and Sheriff followed, and then Albert Senior in his top hat marched alongside Cyril. Behind them, the RFC and other military men marched silently. The men along the road doffed their caps and stood silently.

Flora and Lol awaited them at the front of a packed St Mary's Church. Many had brought flowers which wreathed the church in a bright tribute. Nottingham saluted her bravest ever son.

Flora only knew he was lost to her forever.

20.

All the days from then…

199

She went just once to see him. She finally got to see Albert's corner of a foreign field. It was many years later, her hair had grown white and her son took her. James led her to the grave by the arm and then left her there. She took out her little trowel and planted a single rose from her garden on the grave. The grave was his father's taste, big and black and brooding. It was surrounded by simple wooden crosses. The sunlight fell in rays through the morning mist. There was stillness. She became aware of all that had passed, all the years he had missed. She had hoped to find his ghost here, but it never came.

For so many years, she had missed him so deeply. The life that was stolen from her had hurt her so much. Then gradually the twenties overtook her and she danced and sang again. She never forgot him, but she grew a long way from him. She married and became Mrs Flora Cavanagh Thornhill of Thorpe Le Soken., Essex. Her son, James, became a Captain, but she would not let him fly. Fortunately, he was too young for the second war. She never sang Albert's song again but she grew gardens of her own. She grew roses and chrysanthemums.

Now as she planted this red rose above him, she hummed that song again, just once more. A single teardrop fell on the black marble. The haunting tremolo voice became young again, Flora Young again. He had not grown old like she had. Age had not wearied him nor the years condemned. At the going down of each day's sun and in the morning, she remembered him.

Albert Senior went on to be Mayor of Nottingham a further three times. He did everything he could, throughout the rest of his life, to eternalise his son's memory. He visited France as soon as the war ended and met Cecille. He paid her family to tend the grave he built there for Albert and they still do, although Cecille's grandson does it now. Albert Senior built a small memorial garden on the spot where Cecille had held his son. Sir Albert Ball also went on to live through the second war and was proud of the way Albert was used as an example for the Battle of Britain pilots. He died in 1946.

Lady Harriet Ball never recovered from the shock of her son's death. She retreated into her family and led her life less publicly. She lived through three weeks of a repeated private hell when Cyril went missing after just a few weeks in France. When the announcement came through that he had been taken prisoner, she could only half believe it. The family knew not to speak of Albert's death around her, right up until the day she died, in 1931.

Cyril's career with the RFC in France lasted for just two weeks, before he was shot down and taken prisoner. Cyril was repatriated in 1918. He returned to Albert's old firm on Castle Boulevard for a while. In 1956 he built an engineering works on the site of the family tennis court at Sedgeley. The house was divided into apartments at this time. Cyril flew with the Nottingham Aero Club at Hucknall aerodrome for a while. He succeeded his father in becoming a Councillor, for the Meadows ward of Nottingham in 1947 and died after a short illness in 1958.

Lol married Lieutenant George S. Anderson on March 2nd 1918. Flora was one of the bridesmaids. She had little to do with the Ball family after that. Lol named her eldest son Albert, after her brother. He joined the RAF and flew spitfires in the Second war. He was forced to bale out above the sea near the isle of Kos and died there. Lol ended up sharing the fate of her mother, her cherished son falling from the air and not returning.

Arthur Rhys Davis earned the nickname 'The second Ball'. He went on to run up over twenty victories including that of the German ace, Werner Voss. He was killed in combat in October 1917 and has no known grave. Gerald Maxwell survived the war and ran up 26 victories. He became a Wing Commander in the RAF during World War Two. He died, an old man, in 1969. Cecil Lewis flew in China for a while then moved on to become a writer. He died in 1997, aged 99. In a prolific career as a writer and poet, he was awarded an academy award. More than eight thousand allied airmen lost their lives in the First World War.

Lothar Von Richtofen outlived his older brother and survived the war with forty victories, but was killed whilst piloting a passenger aircraft near Hamburg in 1922.

The names of Thrale, Ball and Holmes are together again on the war memorial in Lenton. Behind it stand the Albert Ball Memorial cottages, built by Albert Senior. The first cross the Germans used to mark Albert's grave can still be seen in the Chapel at Trent College. They have an Albert Ball scholarship and once a year their hockey teams compete for the Albert Ball cup.

In 2003, the children of Annouellin were asked to choose a new name for their junior school. They could have chosen a French football player or politician, but they chose a better example to follow. Now they attend the Collége Albert Ball.

Beneath the Castle, overlooking the city of Nottingham stands Ball's statue. Boom Trenchard opened it in 1921 at a ceremony Flora attended. It is made of grey marble they carved him standing where he belongs, with the wind in his face, up in the air. Flora died in 1985. She was 87 years old when she flew to join her Albert.

203

Printed in Great Britain
by Amazon.co.uk, Ltd.,
Marston Gate.